To Gary

Poor

Jeffrey

*Good luck in your new job
and best wishes*

Paul Flewitt

Paul Flewitt

Edited by
Patti Geesey

Cover Design by
Richard Van Ekeren

Shawthing Publications

Introduction

I read a lot of horror now I have opened my doors to new (and established) authors. I am sent a handful of titles to read a month and, I'll be honest, they're getting a little *meh*. *Meh* being a technical term for *not very interesting*. It seems in this day and age people believe horror only involves serial killers - the type of people you see walking down the road in every day life who wear a metaphorical mask during the daylight and reveal their true selves by night. Whilst this sort of horror does exist - and can make for a good story when done correctly - it seems as though creative types have forgotten the kind of horror that was prevalent in the eighties. It was horrible, that was the point, but it also felt different in the way it took you to different worlds and characters you couldn't possibly hope to meet in real life; characters such as *Jeffrey*.

'Poor Jeffrey' is a reprint of Paul Flewitt's novel, his debut one at that. It hasn't changed from the previous version other than having another run-through for grammar and punctuation. Paul was adamant that he didn't want to tighten it up (where *he* believed it could have been). This was his first novel and he wanted it to stand as such so people can see a very obvious progression as he continues his writing career. And you know what, that takes balls. Given half a chance, if authors are being reprinted, they would grab the chance to tidy their work up or write it using all the techniques they have learned since writing for the first time. God knows I do not dare look back at works I have previously written. I know I have improved ten-fold and know I'd be deeply embarrassed by my first pieces! How's that for an advert for my back catalogue?

Paul Flewitt is a breath of fresh-air in today's horror community. An excellent writer in his own right, with a vivd imagination that pulls you in from the get go, he is often compared to Clive Barker and Mr. Barker's influence is obvious. Again, not a bad thing. And - with that in mind - Clive Barker once said, 'Be yourself. Avoid self-censorship. Love your failures.' It's a quote that stuck in my mind and one that I wonder as to whether Paul read it himself too? Does he regard 'Poor Jeffrey' as a failure because he can see where it should be improved? If that is the case - I long to see what Paul considers a success because 'Poor Jeffrey' is anything but a failure. A story that grips you from page one and throttles you until you've finished can never be considered that. Personally, and I know I am not alone, I can't wait to see what Paul comes up with next. Especially after I challenged him to write a book out of his comfort zone when we met at a convention. Here is a guy who's first book proves one hell of an imagination and a love for the written word… Let's see what this son of a bitch has up his sleeve.

Until then, I present to you his debut… I present 'Poor Jeffrey'.

And I could not be any prouder.

Matt Shaw

Acknowledgements

With a new imprint comes a new set of people to thank. These are the people who helped make this release possible.

First and always, thanks to my wife and children. Without you guys I wouldn't be here writing this page; your patience with my writing moods knows no bounds.

Thanks always go to Patti Geesey, my editor and literary partner in crime, always ready for late night conversations about things like voodoo rituals and dark magic. Your red pen will be legendary.

Thank you to Matt Shaw for everything. Your belief in me has often been greater than my own. You're a rock star!

To everyone that has been supportive of this work in its past guises and to all the people who have appeared in this section for different impressions of this work, thanks. You all know who you are by now.

And lastly, but also most importantly, thank YOU for buying and reading my book. I hope that I entertain you for a short while; enough for you to come back and visit my hearth again … sweet dreams.

This work is dedicated to my grandmother

Georgina Theresa Flewitt

"That which can be imagined, need never be lost."
Clive Barker

Poor Jeffrey couldn't get anything quite right. His father called him stupid, not unkindly, but it was an unfair label; Jeffrey was never stupid. Clumsy, yes, stupid, never. He had clumsy hands, and was tall and gangly with overlong arms, and feet that were somehow always too big in his sneakers. These peculiarities of anatomy meant he would trip over pretty much anything from the telephone stand in the hall to a pesky rock jutting out of the ground. Pretty much anything that a normal foot would merely guide its owner over without harm or incident, Jeffrey's clown-like feet would lead him to some minor catastrophe or other. He had often thought his entire body was ungainly. Never had he considered his foot might be homicidal.

He daydreamed a lot, which didn't help his cause. He could often walk right past his destination because some mathematical problem or fruity teen fantasy had taken hold of his mind and blinded him to the road. It's what killed him in the end. Walking home one night and not looking where he was going, head lost in the memory of the Ouija he and his friends had played with that night. He slipped in the remains of a raccoon or some such road kill, his feet unerringly leading him to the one obstacle in his path that might bring him to ruin.

He couldn't blame the weather for what was about to befall him; it was a cloudless summer evening, the sweet smell of pine mingling with freshly turned earth filling his nostrils. He drifted off to one of those other places he often found

1

himself going to in his mind, heedless of the road by his side. He never noticed the two pinprick lights growing in the distance, just walked with his head down, looking but sightless as he made his mechanical way h

ome. First he felt something slimy underfoot, like rain-slicked mud all smooth and without purchase. Then time seemed to slow for him as he saw headlights rushing toward him. Jeffrey saw his arms pin wheeling to stop a fall that was by now inevitable. In his mind he saw many possible outcomes from his predicament, but it was all happening much too quickly to act any more decisively than to swing his arms and hope. Then he was falling too sharply to recover his balance. He fell hard.

It wouldn't have been fatal, but a truck was passing by at that same instant. The vehicle only struck a passing blow, but it was enough to kill him. But poor Jeffrey, clumsy Jeffrey. He couldn't even get dying quite right.

****

Tommy Sadler sat on the wall outside school and lit another cigarette, steeling himself for what was to come once he got inside. He wiped at his tear-streaked eyes with the back of his hand as he inhaled and enjoyed the smoke burn at the back of his throat. He sat alone, which was unusual. The girls, Chloe and Jade, would likely have been given some kind of dispensation in light of the news.

Tommy, Chloe, and Jade had been Jeffrey's closest

friends; Chloe closest of all. It had become common knowledge that Chloe and Jeffrey had become an item in recent months, but they had known each other most of their lives. Except Jade, of course … she had arrived later. Perhaps the principal of the school had sent Chloe home already and Jade had accompanied her. Perhaps she was too upset to stay in school. The news of Jeffrey's death would be such a shock for her.

Thoughts of that news brought fresh tears to Tommy's eyes. He had tried to put any thoughts of Jeffrey's death out of his mind.

He had been woken by his mother that morning. That in itself should have set alarm bells off in his head. The routine was that his mother would go off to work and leave him to be roused by his radio alarm; it was an arrangement that suited them both since she wouldn't have the irritation of trying to wake him, and he could get a few extra minutes drifting in his dreams. Not that morning. His mother bled into his dreams; first as a distant echo on some imagined breeze, then as a more steadily solidified and tangible form as she spoke into his mind's wandering. He blinked through sleep-blurred eyes until his mind caught up with his body and realised its owner was awake.

"Tommy, I am so sorry," she began as he rose to full alertness, the look in her eyes belying the significance of the message she'd brought. "Tyrone Kinsey was just on the phone. Last night … Jeffrey was killed."

"No." It was the only word he was capable of uttering for

a good while. He sat up in bed, numb. No tears came, not then. His mother held him a little, her need to give comfort greater than his need. He allowed her to stroke his hair and console him but was glad when she left so he could try to better understand his feelings. Half of him thought it was a joke. Jeffrey and he had often laughed about dark and morbid things; they thought they could, given their shared past. Surely this must just be some tasteless prank?

He spent the rest of the morning in that numbness, dressing, and then eating a breakfast he had no appetite for; reading the front page news about the death of his best friend. Even that somehow seemed unreal.

It wasn't until he began the walk to school that the reality seemed to hit him like a sledgehammer. The realisation that he had never taken this morning walk alone, the shock of Jeffrey's absence in his usual morning spot on the porch waiting for him to come out. It had been the same routine throughout his life. No more. That set the tears rolling, the empty hole opening up from the pit of his stomach to his throat. No way to be rid of a hole like that except to weep it out. And so he did.

He walked around for a long time, not wanting to go to the school house and face his sympathetic peers. Few cared much for him, or for Jeffrey, but like their parents they would paint on fake concern and play their part. He knew that it would make him sick to feel such fakery. Tommy knew that neither he nor Jeffrey were hated, but both were treated with a kind of detached resentment, and for them to treat him any other way now would be a lie. If he were to face that now he would likely explode, spit in their faces, and yell at them to tell the damn truth—if they didn't love Jeffrey in life then don't pretend to mourn him in death. All Tommy wanted at this moment was truth. And so he walked into the woods where he and his friends hung around, and remembered.

There was solace in memories. He could hide in memories forever, like he did sometimes in his favourite books. "When the world gets rough … get out" was his mantra; one that he had stuck to since the death of his brother. That would not be possible this time.

Tommy wept fresh tears as he realised that he was likely the last person to see Jeffrey alive. He hadn't even wanted to go out, but Tommy had persuaded him. The girls wanted to party, but Jeffrey had to study. He had an exam coming up. They all did, but Jeffrey would be the only one that would get a grade. That was how it worked. If he hadn't talked Jeffrey round and coaxed him from his bedroom then his friend would never have been hit by a truck. If Tommy hadn't done a lot of things then a lot of other things might not have happened, either.

When they were nine years old, had Tommy not wanted to try to swing on the old tyre swing that went out over Kiddlebrook stream, then Jeffrey wouldn't have near drowned and spent the Easter holidays in bed with pneumonia and a broken arm from a bad fall. Had Tommy not wanted to go try to steal an apple from Haggerty's orchard then maybe Jeffrey wouldn't have had his legs painted green for a week from rubbing them with dock leaves after running through a huge patch of stinging nettles. It seemed whatever Tommy persuaded Jeffrey to do ended in some kind of chaos or disaster.

As he walked through the woods, he thought, *What would Jeff do?* It was a question he had often asked during times of indecision; after all, of all his friends, Jeffrey was probably the wisest. For his age, of course. Tommy had almost come to mischief on many occasions, but for Jeffrey's last minute words of reason. It seemed that it was what Jeffrey was there for … reason.

And that was when his brain started racing toward a way to make things right. He would do what Jeffrey always did and find a solution. Who knew what that would mean in the end?

Now he sat and smoked his cigarette, finally giving up on Chloe and Jade arriving. Tommy jumped down off the wall and ran his hand through his dark hair. Perhaps the girls were already there, waiting in their accustomed spot by the lockers. Having already run the gamut of condolences. Having already put on the fake smile and thanked the fakers for their mockery of concern.

For a second, Tommy smiled; he was forming a plan.

****

Jack Coltraine lurked in the playground all day, watching the comings and goings, tuning in to the mothers' and fathers' conversations. He had been watching for days now, learning the routines of the families in the town. Today he would have to strike. He was hungry.

Scenes like these did not bring back any memories of childhood playgrounds for him; he had very few memories from his youth. For him, life began sometime in his teens. He had paid a king's ransom in psychiatrists' fees to unlock the memories that would show him his childhood, all to no avail.

He had paperwork, which told him of parents too young to care for him, yet they told him nothing of who he was. It was just a tragic story to his ears but bore no relation to the person he had become. He was his own construct, not some fall-out from a tragic event from his past. He barely thought about his life before his hunger anymore. It didn't matter.

He was evil. That was the long and short of it. He had been put on the earth, at this point in time, to do the things that he had done. He was not crazy; no end of psychiatrists and psychoanalysts had confirmed that. He was a perfectly sane man. Therefore, the only conclusion was that he was evil, plain and simple. It was a label he adored, he reveled in it. He was a predator among a sea of cattle, his function to devour. Of course, he would tell himself that he was keeping these creatures safe … in the safest place there was. The truth was that he was doing what the world would do to them eventually anyway … turning them to shit.

Evening came on chilly and he zipped up his overcoat as he walked over to where the last child sat. He had named her the "last child" because she always seemed to be the last to leave, always alone; she was an easy target. He watched far longer than his hunger usually allowed him; he had to be certain that he could do the deed unseen. Finally, he had waited long enough. Now was the time.

He grabbed her from behind, clapping a hand over her mouth. She did not scream; she couldn't. She had been born a mute. He watched her passing notes to her friends and using sign language with those who understood it. Covering her mouth was mere habit, a part of the ritual. He swept her up easily and tucked her under his arm. Never breaking his stride for a beat, he marched away from the ground, hand fluttering in an approximation of the sign language he'd watched her use. He bundled her into the passenger seat of his car and drove away unnoticed, unseen. No one cared.

****

Tyrone Kinsey had arrived home early in the morning and sat up until his wife fell into a fitful sleep. He knew her rest wouldn't last long by the way she mumbled and moaned, her eyes roving behind their lids. She was troubled, what mother wouldn't be.

The call from Sheriff Davies had come a few hours earlier, the call that every parent dreads from the moment their child begins to walk. Marie had dropped to her knees in the kitchen as the sheriff told her that her son was dead. Her mouth opened wide and she rocked backward and forward, silently screaming her despair. It broke Tyrone's heart.

8

He had gone along to the hospital to see his son, to identify the body. Marie had insisted on joining him and Tyrone didn't argue. He was running on autopilot, being strong for the good of his wife. Tears would come later. He looked down on the gurney as the sheet was drawn back and saw his son lying there, holding his wife up as her legs buckled once more.

It had taken hours to get Marie to sleep a little. Every time her eyes fluttered closed, a dream would jolt her back to wakefulness and the realisation of her loss would hit her all over again. All Tyrone could do was hold her close and wipe her tears.

Once she was asleep, he drove up to the eastern fields and made a pretence of looking over the fences around his land, knocking in a few nails and replacing one or two sections that looked rotten. If some sections were not replaced correctly, what did it matter? They were his fences, after all.

He looked down over his land, in his mind seeing his sons running through the tall grasses, giggling. He could almost hear the sound of them echoing up the valley toward him. He wondered what had gone so wrong. Just a few scant years before, everything had been as he had dreamed it would be. He had taken over the land from his father, he had married the woman he loved and had two sons who were growing into fine young men. He dreamed that one day soon one of them would take his place and stand where he now stood, looking down over his lands and marveling at the perfection of it all. Except that now it wasn't perfect and all he had were the memories of two boys running in the long grasses.

He looked up at the cloudless sky, and sighed. There was no breeze that early morning, not a single sigh of wind. It would be a stifling day to come. It almost felt like the world had taken a breath … and still held it.

****

After school, and the expected hell of a thousand fakers, Tommy went right home. Neither Chloe nor Jade had shown up to school and he wasn't surprised. Jeffrey, Chloe, and Tommy were lifelong friends. They had been inseparable since they were tiny toddlers, their mothers watching them crawl on the lawn together as they sat on the porch drinking iced tea. Lately though, Jeffrey and Chloe had drawn a little closer; their friendship had grown to something much more. Tommy hadn't spoken to her or Jade since Jeffrey's death the previous night, yet he couldn't seem to bring himself to make a call or visit the house. He knew the grief that he felt would be magnified many times in Chloe, by virtue of their closeness. That thought lent fuel to his search for a solution. Success came from the unlikeliest source.

In recent months, maybe almost a year, his friends had taken an interest in magical teachings. They had spent many nights in the woods with a Ouija marked out and a bottle of liquor at their side. Jade had become quite adept at reading tarot over the last few months. It was almost a game to them, to imagine themselves great seers. Tommy had bought a library of magical teachings and demonic articles, which he read to the others to spook them. It was all good fun! Now those games took on new significance.

Under his bed, Tommy kept his special books, writings that he wouldn't want his mother to see. Among the skin magazines with their blonde bombshells and other detritus of a teenage boy's life was his box. Inside was the book that may just hold the solution to his problem.

As he took out the box, his hand trembled a little. He was scared to open the little chest and find that he had no hope. In the end, all he had was hope.

****

The death of Jeffrey Kinsey hit Chloe harder than she might ever have expected. Perhaps a few short months ago she would have been able to accept it easier but not now. Things had changed between them and now she couldn't bear to consider a life that did not include Jeffrey. Her Jeffrey.

Of course, his death would have been a shock at any point in her life. She had been very good friends with Jeffrey and Tommy for as long as she could remember. As youngsters they played together on the lawns of their houses and that relationship had continued all through school. In the summer months, when school was out, they would gather in the woods and wander the country around town making whatever limited mischief they could. In school they were inseparable too. Wherever the boys led, Chloe would follow in utter bemusement at their horseplay. Their lust for fun was charming and it drew her into their games. She had a certain need to see what they would do, and what Jeffrey would have to talk Tommy out of next.

Chloe was very self-conscious around the boys. As she got older she began to notice changes about her that were not happening to the boys; she was getting wide hips and her breasts were beginning to grow exponentially. She was so aware of these changes that she began to take action against her body, first wearing baggy shirts, then binding her growing bosom with bandages to make herself as flat chested as she could. She continued to do that until Jade showed up in her make-up and skirts, showing her that it wasn't only the bitchy town girls who felt the need to revel in their sexuality. Jade seemed to like the attention that some people gave her. She wouldn't ever admit to such an enjoyment, in fact she would affect an air of distaste and brush of the attention as if it wasn't such a big thing. Chloe learned how to be a girl around Jade and was thankful for it. Thankful also that her beloved boys, Tommy and Jeffrey, didn't judge her and never made mention of her growing maturity. They had become like her family in a way that her actual blood sisters couldn't ever be, and much more than that, she loved both the boys like brothers she had never had. They looked out for each other.

In recent months, though, her feelings for Jeffrey had deepened. Her maturing psyche had become drawn to his wisdom and his vulnerability. She enjoyed their conversations and valued his opinions on most subjects. Then, one night, she took the initiative and kissed him long and sweetly. He seemed confused at first, like he couldn't get his lips to respond and she feared that her feelings were not shared, but after a moment's awkwardness he responded as keenly as she had hoped he might.

From then she had dared to dream; to dream of a future with Jeffrey, of university, and maybe sometime in the distant future, marriage and children.

Now her tears could not be denied. As soon as her mother told her the news of Jeffrey's death, they came and she could not seem to stop them. School had called to offer their sympathies and assure her that they would understand her absence, and Jade had visited and stayed around trying to console her with little success. Grief had taken hold of her heart in a cold grip and was unshakeable.

She needed a way to find a sort of peace with what had occurred; she had to find a way to stop her heart from breaking clean in two and killing her. It would take time; perhaps, she might always feel the loss of Jeffrey. For now there seemed no importance in thinking about the future. All there was for her now was grief, tears, and heart rending loss. And it hurt like crazy.

****

Jade walked home that evening exhausted. Consoling Chloe

through her suffering was tiring work, but she couldn't bring herself to resent her for her indulgence as she might have done with some of her friends back in the city.

Of the four friends that she had in the town, Chloe was the one who first offered her a hand. Jeffrey had tried and failed, Jade misunderstanding his kindness for something more sexual. It didn't take long for her to be disabused of the notion as she saw the way Chloe grew ever closer to him. Jade had then tried to start some kind of romance with Tommy, but her attempts were futile. He was not in the frame of mind to love himself, never mind her. So she luxuriated in the warm glow of friendships she could never have forged in the city. Now that was all going to change with the death of one of their number; it had to. It made her sad to think of the group so incomplete, but she couldn't bring herself to weep for the loss. It was never her style to cry.

Jade wandered home and tried to order her thoughts and feelings. She had gone no further than a few yards from Chloe's door when Tommy appeared at her side. Jade jumped but he didn't snigger as he usually would, just fell in step with her and walked with her. "How's Chloe?" he asked clumsily.

"Terrible, why not go see for yourself?"

"Nah ... don't think I could face her right now," he replied with a shrug.

"She'd want to see you, though," Jade insisted.

"I guess, but ... not yet."

"Why? She is your friend."

"I know that, but ... bad memories, dude ... it hurts."

14

"You think Chloe isn't hurting?"

"I know that she is."

"So go see her then. Just give her a hug and let her know you care, eh?"

"Yeah … just not tonight. I have things I need to do," Tommy said, seeming distracted.

"What things, Tommy? Are you okay?" Jade asked, noting his haunted expression.

"I'm fine. I just need to figure this out. Look, I gotta run. I'll speak with you guys later … tomorrow, maybe."

"Where are you going now?" Jade asked.

"Things to do, I already said."

"Well … okay," Jade replied, uncertain. "I'll call you tomorrow."

He nodded and shrugged a little non-committal as he walked away from her. He didn't say goodbye.

She watched after him, wondering about the state he must be in. She hadn't considered Tommy throughout the day, so wrapped up in Chloe's emotions had she been. Looking at him now though, it looked like someone had hollowed to the core of him. It was sad to see the usually so gregarious Tommy so visibly devastated. She made it her mission to watch out for him, to walk down any path he chose, just to ensure that he was safe. After all, that had been Jeffrey's role in her little group, and he was gone.

****

The town was unused to tragedy. Nothing ever happened in their tranquil corner of the world, save for the annual gala and the parade, which would wend its way through the town. As far as excitement went, that was the pinnacle. Anything more and the town itself was in uproar. That was the state it was in upon the news of Jeffrey Kinsey's death, followed quickly by the disappearance of a young girl from the municipal park. Things like these just did not happen here. So the town got itself busy with preparations for the Kinsey funeral, which would likely see the entire populace turn out to pay their respects, just as they had to the poor boy's brother. The Kinseys were an old family in the town and their loss was the loss of the entire town. The hurt was shared, as was the anger over the disappearance of the little girl.

In his office, Sheriff Davies contemplated the events of the past week or so and despaired a little. He thought he'd left such dark events in the city when he'd left it, but no. Here it was once again, that darkness, dogging him.

He rubbed his knuckles into his eyes and when he looked up again his wife was before him, hot coffee in one hand and a bagel in the other. He smiled wanly as she cleared a space on his cluttered desk and set down his refreshments. "You work too hard, Klimpt," she admonished him.

"I have to, honey ... things are looking serious right now." He sighed.

"I haven't seen you this tired since we moved out here. You're too old for this kind of thing ... kids dying and disappearing. It's not for you these days, old man."

"But it says sheriff on my door. While it says that, I've got no choice. Investigations have to happen, statements … you know how it is?"

"I know … but I don't approve. You are almost sixty years old, Klimpt Davies. Time to hang up that holster of yours and spend some time in the garden with the plants and the dog." She smiled sheepishly.

"And I will … promise. After this has died down, I'll hand in the badge and that will be that. Let me just find this girl safe first," he said, looking gravely into his wife's eyes.

"Well, what kind of wife would I be if I didn't let you play shining knight, eh? You find that girl, get her home safe to her mother, then you bring yourself home safe to me, you promise?" she said, taking his hand.

"That I do, girl," he replied.

Later Klimpt Davies would reflect on this conversation and the only promise that he would ever make again was that he would make no more promises. The events unfolding in his town were soon to lose control and no one involved would ever be the same again. Some wouldn't even survive them.

****

Frank Fielding dressed in his best black suit and polished his shoes to a high shine. He'd spent the last few days reading the papers, raging at the happenings going on within feet of his own doorstep. Never in his fifty-some years had he felt insecure in the town. This was *his* town. He had been born here. It was the kind of place where people lived, grew old, and died. People did not get abducted in this serene part of the world; people did not get run down on the interstate. It just didn't happen. Yet now both those heinous things had happened in the space of a week and it didn't sit comfortably with him.

Frank was the wealthiest man in the town, the largest land owner and biggest benefactor in the area. His great grandfather, grandfather, and his father had spent their whole lives building the business and their level of respectability just so that Frank could know the life he'd lived so far. They lay now in one of the biggest family burial plots in the churchyard ... there was even a Fielding Street in town! Rumour had it he would be mayor in the town before too long and it was his intention to run for the office, too. It felt like it was his right to do so. He had no doubts that he would be elected, either.

For now, Frank raged at the injustice of the terrible things that were happening in his world. He slipped on his jacket and set out for Tyrone Kinsey's house, to help Ty and his wife fix their house in preparation for the burial of their son. After that he would figure out how to help in the search for the little girl and he would call on the good sheriff with an offer of men and money. He would do anything to put right what was awry in his town. It was his duty.

****

Jade and Chloe walked through the trees, following the sound of music that emanated from somewhere deeper in the wood. They knew where they were going; it was the usual meeting place for them, and this event had been arranged for a little while now.

They stepped into a clearing after a little way and saw Tommy, a bottle of something in his hand and a joint held between his lips. He smiled as the girls approached and did not complain when Jade took the joint from him and inhaled deeply.

"I'm glad you both came. It kinda means a lot to me." Tommy spoke hesitantly, almost as if unsure of his words and choosing them with care.

"We weren't gonna miss this, were we?" Jade smiled.

"It's for Jeff. Of course we came," Chloe said, taking Tommy in a short embrace. "I missed you lately, Tommy. What have you been doing?"

Tommy looked her in the eye, then quickly away again. "I'm sorry, Chloe. I should've come to see you," he said plainly.

"Yes, you should have. But that's okay. Are you all right?" Chloe asked.

"I'm getting there. Look, enough of this bullshit, huh? Can we just party already?" he said, his face breaking into a grin that never touched his eyes.

"But of course … lead us to the refreshments." Jade chuckled.

Throughout the night, the three toasted the memory of

their friend half-heartedly and spoke about old times. Jade mostly listened to Tommy's and Chloe's stories of their distant past, their childhood and the things they'd done as youngsters. Jade felt envious of their adventures; having grown in the city she had no tales such as these, just assorted horror stories from the ghettos where she went to school.

The sun was beginning to rise, turning the sky a purplish colour, when they finally decided to head home. That was when Tommy spoke.

"Look, if I had a plan that sounded kinda weird, you'd hear me out, right?"

"When did you not say weird things, Tommy?" Chloe giggled.

"I'm bein' serious. I got an idea, but … it's kinda weird."

"What is it, Tommy?" Jade asked, brows knitted together.

"I can't say, not right now. I need to read some more. But I got a plan for when they bury Jeff," he said.

"What kinda plan?" Chloe asked sharply.

"I'll tell you if I think it'll work," he said, and then left them to walk back to town alone.

****

Chloe dreamed she was nine years old. It was summer and the sun was high in the cloudless blue sky. Bees buzzed around and butterflies went from wildflower to wildflower, chasing the bees for the ripest flowers. She knew a feeling of utter contentment that afternoon, sitting under a shady tree with a book in her lap.

Suddenly, she heard a snigger from somewhere behind and to the left. A second later and she was drenched from head to foot in freezing water. Raucous laughter echoed over the field as the two boys ran giggling across the brook and into the neighbouring pasture.

"Tommy Saddler, I'm gonna tell your father what you did!" she yelled after the boys. "You, too, Jeffrey Kinsey!"

Tommy turned at the sound of her voice and looked at her with a sheepish grin on his face. "You would too, wouldn't ya," he yelled across the river.

"You know I would," she snapped.

"Aww hell ... you gotta admit it was funny." Tommy simpered.

"You're not the one dripping wet," she returned.

"It's only a little water, Chloe," Jeffrey said. He had come slowly to Tommy's side.

"It's cold, stinky river water ... I could catch a disease."

"Well, if you were gonna catch a disease I figure Tommy and I woulda already caught it first," Jeffrey reasoned.

"I doubt it. You're boys and you're always in the water," Chloe shot back.

"So then ... we haven't caught no diseases yet," Tommy said proudly.

"You probably did. You just didn't notice," she returned.

Tommy crossed the river by a bunch of stepping stones and sniffed Chloe's hair and face. He wrinkled his nose as he looked at her. "You're right. It is stinky water," he said, barely able to suppress a giggle.

Chloe looked him in the eyes, mouth agape and lost for words for a second, then she pushed him in the chest. His laugh faltered and died as he realised he was going to topple backward. He couldn't stop his momentum as he pin wheeled his arms madly in an effort to stay upright. Finally, he went over with a splash into the river. He coughed and spluttered for a second, trying to fight his way to his feet again. Chloe burst into crazy laughter when he finally climbed from the river and looked at her glumly, water dripping from his hair and pouring from the tops of his shoes. She looked over at Jeffrey and saw that he was rolling on the floor and holding his sides, totally incapable of controlling his mirth.

Chloe's dream-self laughed along with them, even as she felt herself being pulled backward and away from the scene. As often happens in dreams, she felt herself flying through the air. Thick mists all around meant that guessing her destination was impossible, so she gave herself over to the dream and enjoyed the ride.

She appeared to be in the town, Tommy and Jeffrey standing on either side of her. They had just been to the store and bought drinks and some sweets. Jeffrey and Tommy were counting up what money they had remaining between them. This was a different summer, maybe a year later. She watched as they wandered down the street, knowing what would happen next.

The three got as far as the street corner when three older boys appeared from the back of Henrietta's. Tommy looked up as the shadows of the boys loomed over them. Chloe heard him take a sharp breath in; the sound made Jeffrey look up, too.

"What ya got there, kid? Stack o' dimes?" The biggest leered. "Mamma gave you your allowance, huh?"

The three younger kids averted their eyes and tried to walk around the group, an unspoken decision made between them to try to get out of this potentially dangerous situation in one piece. They knew Glenn Herbert and Carl Spratt. They had been expelled from the school two summers ago, now they spent their time running amok around the area. They were bad boys, everyone knew it. The biggest, Carl, stepped into their path and stopped them from getting away. "I asked you a question." He leered again. "Did Mamma give you your allowance?"

"Yeah," Jeffrey mumbled, not looking Carl in the eye.

"You wanna donate it to my charity?" Carl asked.

"No, thank you," Jeffrey replied and tried again to step around the brute.

"Okay, lemme put it another way … gimme the fucking cash." Carl snarled.

"You leave him alone!" Chloe said, outraged.

"You shut your hole, girly, or I'll fix ya good," Spratt warned. "Gimme your money … all of you!"

Jeffrey looked up and met Carl Spratt's eyes for the first time in the exchange; he saw the malice and madness in the boy's face and made his decision. He held out his hand and offered the money. Spratt reached out to take the few coins and two notes that Jeffrey had left with his attention only on his prize. Suddenly, out of nowhere, Tommy yelled in incoherent rage and threw himself at Carl Spratt, punching and kicking at the bigger boy and growling with each impact. Both fell over onto the street and rolled around a little. By some trick of luck, Tommy found himself on top of the bully. He sat astride the brute's back and began to smash his head into the asphalt, tears streaking his cheeks as he bounced the head from the curb.

It took Chloe, Jeffrey, and Herbert to drag Tommy off the trembling form of Carl Spratt, such was the heat of his rage. Later, all Tommy would say was that he got angry at the way the boy had spoken to Chloe. Much later, he admitted it was that afternoon he had been told of his brother's death.

The scene faded with Tommy's tears, Jeffrey with his arm around his friend in an attempt at comforting him. That was the day their childhood changed.

Chloe was flying through the mists once more. She relaxed into the rhythm of the dream; it brought her some comfort from the grief of her waking life since Jeffrey's death.

The scene that now unfolded was a couple of years on. The sun was again high and hot in a cloudless sky. The three friends were now joined by Jade. She was a stranger still at this point in time, but she was in their circle. Jeffrey had asked Chloe to speak to her, to offer her a friendship. He had tried and been snubbed, Chloe she had seemed to accept gratefully. She was a little brash, a little abrupt, but she was now their friend.

There seemed no point to this scene. The others had been formative times in their friendship, but this seemed to be just another day. They walked to the town line, joking around, talking about school and the latest fads. It was a normal day.

That was when the realisation hit her hard that this was one of the last normal days, one of the last summers that she would spend with this group of beautiful, crazy people. In this scene they went to the woods and played music while they drank and danced like sprites into the evening. At the end of the night, she had looked at Jeffrey and saw a person that was the boy she knew, but somewhere behind his floppy fringe seemed to be someone else peeking out. It would take her another year to figure out what her drunken eyes were trying to tell her that night and in her dreams she cursed her caution.

Her wet pillow and the sunlight slanting through her bedroom window conspired to wake her. She looked through bleary eyes at a summer morning that wasn't anything like the summers she'd dreamed of. This summer day was a mockery of the days she had shared with Jeffrey and Tommy all her life, because she couldn't believe that she would ever feel like she had then, walking between her two friends. It was the morning of Jeffrey's funeral and Chloe had no more tears to cry, so she just lay down and remembered for a while longer.

****

25

Poor Jeffrey

The day of Jeffrey's funeral dawned with the news of the disappearance of the mute girl, news which had broken the hearts of Jeffrey's parents; their thoughts were with the parents of the missing girl even in their own moment of grief. This and other news was roundly discussed by family and close friends who had gathered at the house, waiting for the hearse.

Tragedy was a regular house guest for Tyrone and Marie Kinsey. In recent years they'd had a bad time on the farm, summers too long and hot to give a proper yield meant they had precious little to send to market. Just as times began to look like a change for the couple, their oldest son was killed while on maneuvers with his army unit. That had almost ended Ty, who had stood so proud when he had watched his boy take his silver dollar and march off to defend his country. Now, here they were once again. A normal, happy young couple, now they looked hollowed out by the loss of both their sons. They nodded and accepted the condolences from neighbours and friends, but they looked like automatons going through the motions of normality.

Tommy, Chloe, and Jade had bunked off school to attend the funeral. They looked around nervously at the local dignitaries who were packed like sweating sardines into the small farmhouse. There in the sitting room, glass of scotch in hand, was Frank Fielding; his white suit almost shining in the collection of black mourning dress of the other attendees. In the hallway stood Father Cade awaiting the cars for the family, and waiting for the opportunity to regale any mourner too overcome with emotion about the promise of paradise that lay just beyond the veil. He had no takers at the moment. Scattered around were still others. Sheriff Davies and his wife spoke with Stan Herbert, owner of the local hardware store. Henrietta, the owner of the only bar in town, stood talking to Jenny Harlowe. All in honour of Poor Jeffrey Kinsey.

It had been the girls who had given Jeffrey his nickname: *Poor Jeffrey*. They had watched him since they could remember, bumping into things and tripping over things. Each time, his friends would giggle with him and pat him on the back. *Poor Jeffrey* they would purr as they giggled together. He was a joke, but the understanding was that he was *their* joke. No one else was allowed to laugh.

When the cars came, the Kinseys got in and sat silently as they were transported from the house to the chapel. The cars moved slowly through the town and a few people stopped in the street to watch them pass. Tommy watched them with some distaste, feeling like a fish in a bowl. The same as when his own brother had died.

Jeffrey's group of friends sat at the back of the chapel as they might in the classroom, exchanging hushed conversation. Even though there was a general hum of noise echoing around the stone walls, it still seemed proper to whisper; perhaps out of some perceived reverence for the church or for the deceased. Who could tell which? They stood when Jeffrey's casket, its sides smoothed and varnished to a mirror shine and brass handles gleaming, was carried past with flowers cascading from the lid in tumbles of yellow and white lilies; evidence of the loss that was felt by Jeffrey's passing. The girls sobbed uncontrollably at the sight, as did several of the other ladies in the congregation. The men looked respectfully stern as they stood with heads bowed. Tommy tried to suppress a laugh but was only partly successful, which earned him a smattering of glares from around the room. It was his typical reaction to moments of stoicism; marriages, funerals, and anything which involved a vicar would elicit the same response. The attempt to look respectful while holding in the laugh just made him appear ill. After the service, they followed the other mourners to the graveyard at the back of the church and watched as their friend's body was lowered carefully into the ground. And Poor Jeffrey was gone. No pomp, no fanfare.

Just gone.

The other mourners trailed away and the three teens followed. They attended the funeral supper at the parents' request, offered their awkward, stuttered condolences and then left hurriedly. They had a plan; they thought they knew how to bring that plan to fruition. Still, even with their confidence they went to the woods at the limits of the town to smoke a joint and drink some brandy. The things they had planned took guts that none of the three were certain they possessed.

****

Jack Coltraine wasn't his real name of course; it was just a convenient alias. It amused him to carry identification similar to someone with celebreté while he did what he was doing. And so famous jazz saxophonists, bluesmen, and long forgotten actors had been seemingly put to work on farms and in factories all over the country; it was his perverse joke on a society that had seemingly forgotten its greatest artists. That was why he chose his favourites, so their names might live on a little longer. He had washed up in this small town quite by accident, but he wasn't one to let accidents get in his way.

These were the kinds of opportunities he looked for. These were the places he enjoyed inhabiting. It went hand in hand with his use of obscure celebrity names. It was the reason he chose his victims, although that isn't a word he would use for them. He liked to make the faceless famous. It was somehow his calling to do that.

It would be his pleasure to place this anonymous township on the map, even if only for a moment. This old, decrepit house would be just as famous as the charred piece of ground that had once been home to the Gein family once Coltraine had done his work.

He advanced on the little girl and smiled. She hadn't struggled overmuch before and she was much too terrified as he smiled his smile and bent her head slightly to the right. She gasped, just a little, perhaps thinking he was going to kiss her, as he bent and put his lips to her little neck, feeling her useless vocal chords under his touch. He paused for just a second, savouring the smell and heat, then he bit down into her flesh as hard as he was able until blood spurted into his mouth and down his throat.

Warm and sickly sweet, he sucked and swallowed down the nectar before he tore away the flesh. He barely chewed the meat in his eagerness for fulfillment. His meal had begun and his hunger abated with each bloody mouthful. He slowed his progress after a while. He wanted to enjoy the slimy, almost slug-like texture of the meat as it slid down his throat eagerly, like it desired nothing more than to be in his stomach. Blood chased the meat, tasting sweeter and sweeter as he worked his way through the meal, like ambrosia to his palette. He chewed and suckled, turning his face a deep burgundy colour after a while.

He enjoyed her silence. She hadn't struggled at all during his meal making. Only the quickened breaths still getting shallower gave her the impression of life and he could imagine her as a china doll. She had looked at him with wide eyes, inquisitive rather than fearful. She intrigued him. It would hurt him if she had been able to cry out in terror, the ones who did that always broke his heart just a little. He barely noticed as her body convulsed, her back arched, and her feet jittered around momentarily as he drained her blood into himself. Finally, her body expired and she went limp in his arms but he didn't notice that, either. For a moment he thought he might be raised up and achieve some state of nirvana, attain some sense of being filled up and made whole somehow. A place of sweet song and bright light, for a second he saw ...

But here she was and he was in the same dark room with its damp walls and rotten boards. There was no sound here; just a pure void, which held only the diner and his plate.

When he was full and the mute girl long since dead, he calmly washed the blood from his hands and face. Then he took the girl out beyond the limits of the town, almost to the state line, and left her in a comfortable spot by a stream just a little way from the road. He arranged her hair in a fan, like a halo around her head. It was the only concession to kindness he would make. Perhaps her remains would be found sooner or later. Perhaps they would never be found. Coltraine couldn't care less now. She became cattle at the moment of her death. Even the fact he had come so close to whatever state it was that he wanted to reach wouldn't raise her in his estimation. She had failed him utterly. Her purpose was now served.

****

Poor Jeffrey, he hadn't even died properly. He had felt the truck hit him, felt himself being flung around by the force of the impact. Then he seemed to be jolted out of his body. After a few seconds of disorientation, he realised he was seeing the scene from a way down the road. He watched the driver approach his body like a live wire or a spitting cobra, then he heard the man scream fit to burst as he realised what he'd done. Poor guy. He watched as medics worked on his body and very quickly decided that their labours were an exercise in futility. After they'd bundled his body up and packed him off into the mortician's van, he was left alone. He felt no compunction to follow his body; what happened to his remains from there on seemed somewhat redundant now that he was dead.

He wondered why he hadn't gone to heaven, though he had never really believed in its existence in life. He wondered as he wandered homeward. *Was this it?* The thought didn't seem entirely unpleasant, to stay around and watch his family live their lives without him. He could maybe watch over his friends, too. Perhaps mess with their heads a little if he caught them at the Ouija or if he could learn to move things like a ghost. *Like a ghost?* He laughed at the thought.

When he arrived home, he wished he hadn't bothered. His mother's grief was unbearable to witness while his father looked hollowed out, unable to comfort his wife. Both sat at the kitchen table with glasses of liquor close to hand. Jeffrey left them to their grief.

And so it had gone for the following week. Jeffrey watching unseen as preparations were made and visitors called with their condolences and that secret wish for a scrap of gossip to take back to town with them as proof of their being good neighbours. He went to the school and watched Tommy, Chloe, and Jade attempt to carry on like nothing at all had happened. It was how they had all tried to appear, indifferent and untouched by the world and its happenstance.

It was a sham, of course. Jeffrey had visited each of their houses and witnessed them mourn him. Perhaps more touching than this was the private memorial the three had held for him. It had been a fine party and Jeffrey had tried, and failed, to make his presence known. His failure didn't depress him, though. It was enough to watch and to know that he was there with them just like always.

The day after the party it became apparent that Jeffrey had missed something. His friends were making plans. He knew the signs, the secret glances; the hurried words as they passed each other in the hall between classes. He had even seen Tommy palm a note to Chloe but couldn't read quickly enough as he peered over her shoulder to find out anything of value. That evening he followed Tommy home. He wanted to keep an eye on him. Maybe it was just a hangover, but Tommy looked unwell.

Nothing seemed unusual at first. Tommy ate dinner with his folks, then glanced at his homework a few times without actually doing anything with it. He took a couple of phone calls from Jade, then went to his room to turn in for the night. Just a normal evening. It was then though, that events turned slightly strange. Jeffrey followed his friend to his room, fully aware that Tommy wouldn't be going to sleep anytime soon no matter what he had told his parents.

Jeffrey watched his friend bend and retrieve a box from under his bed and place it almost reverentially on his desk. Jeffrey knew what the box contained, had even contributed objects to the collection; his heart sank when Tommy pulled out the thing he had desperately not wanted him to. Tommy gasped and hurried to the door, fumbling with the key as he tried to lock it quickly. Clumsy. He could've been caught.

Tommy stripped off his shirt as he went back to the desk and started to flick through the book that Jeffrey had prayed never to see again once it had gone into Tommy's box. It was evil. Jeffrey had sensed that much as soon as Tommy had shown it to him. Tommy had bought the book from a thrift store in the city while on a trip to visit with family. Tommy said the old lady behind the counter never knew where the book had come from, just that it had dropped through the mailbox and been on her shelves ever since. He hadn't paid a dime for the object but the lady had thanked him for taking it from her possession and even wrapped it in paper for him.

It was bound in human skin, Tommy had declared with a morbid delight in his voice, the words handwritten and ancient. The claim on antiquity was solid enough, the stained pages were evidence of its age, but it was the subject matter that had so disturbed Jeffrey. It was a grimoire, an instruction in the arts of the shadows. It had fascinated Tommy as much as it had sickened Jeffrey. What was he doing with it?

Tommy was looking intently at the pages as he flicked through them, his eyes flitting from page to box and back again; checking his stores. Was he planning a working?

Poor Jeffrey, he could do nothing but watch as Tommy nodded to himself and took the silver bladed knife from the box. He studied the page one last time then began his work. First he pressed the blade against the flesh of his chest, just above his left nipple, and began slicing; marking himself with an image from the book.

Jeffrey tried to see what it was but the writing on the pages was tiny. All he could do was watch as Tommy carved the sigil into his chest. After several moments the work there was finished but Tommy did not stop, he took the blade to the opposite side and began carving a second icon which mirrored the first. His hands shook badly now but he completed the task to his satisfaction and set his blade down. He stood and walked to the mirror to admire his handiwork, allowing the blood to trickle down his chest.

Jeffrey stood behind him, horrified.

The following few days were one strangeness after another. His friends hardly went to school in the couple of days before his funeral. They were hanging around in the woods on the town's limits, away from prying eyes. They were planning some sort of ritual, obviously. He had watched Tommy carve more sigils into Chloe and Jade which were similar to his own.

All marked, they flinched when the fabric of clothes brushed against their mutilations. If only he could hear their plans, but they spoke in whispers now, perhaps they always had and he just hadn't noticed.

Then came the night before his funeral. Jeffrey followed Tommy to O'Halloran's farm and watched as his friend drew a pint of blood from a cow, the dark fluid spurting from vein to bowl. It made no complaint and didn't seem adversely affected by the theft, just munched cud as Tommy transferred its blood from his bowl and into a bottle. Jeffrey followed Tommy and watched him hide the blood in the woods, then go home as if all were normal. He smiled at his folks, ate a quick sandwich and watched a little of the ball game with his father. He cheered and growled in the relevant places, then took his leave for bed. Then Jeffrey watched as his friend consulted the grimoire and began slicing at his flesh, across his stomach and down each arm.

He watched all of this in anguish. What were his friends doing? How was he to stop them?

****

"I don't think this is such a great idea, Tommy," Chloe said, passing the joint over to Jade. "I mean, it isn't gonna work, is it?"

Tommy looked over at her over the bottom of his beer bottle. "Of course it's gonna work. I showed you, didn't I?"

"Well ... you showed me some internet stuff ..."

"I showed you proof that this shit is real. Now ... your heart has to be in this, Chloe, or it ain't gonna work. Not even a chance," Tommy warned.

"You want this to happen, don't you?" Jade asked, a frown creasing her brow.

"Of course ... you know I do ... but ..."

"So chill out, Chloe." Jade smiled.

"Look. If it works, it's all cool. If it doesn't, no harm no foul, right?" Tommy shrugged.

"I guess so," Chloe said, a wan smile on her face.

"Jeff would be so freakin into this." Jade giggled, raising

her hands over her head and stretching out.

"Yeah." Tommy giggled. "Yeah, he would."

Chloe sipped more of her drink and began to relax a little. Over the last few days, as Tommy had carved the marks into her flesh, she had begun to have some reservations about Tommy's plan. She knew better than anyone what Tommy's bright ideas could lead to, yet she had said nothing. In her mind it was just going to be a game, nothing more. Jade had assured her of it.

"This is gonna be the biggest thing we ever tried, can you imagine?" Jade asked the wind.

"Can't you feel the magic in the air?" Tommy laughed.

"Stop making fun of me." Jade admonished him, though she giggled at the same time.

"C'mon … time to go," Tommy announced, standing up to leave. "Time to get the real party started."

****

Coltraine sat and quietly ate his sandwich, fighting to keep each mouthful down against a system that only wanted to reject it. He had chosen ham because it was closest to his favoured choice of flesh, yet his rebellious stomach was wise to his trickery and carried on with its convulsions. Beside his last meal, this meat was putrescent, rotting, but a working man must eat. He laughed and joked absently along with the other guys on his work detail but his mind was elsewhere. His mind was on meat, raw and red. On dark arteries sparkling and spurting, filled with sweet blood. On the slowly fading pulse. His mind wandered over to the kills, the moment of attaining his meal and the confusion in their eyes as he stole them from the world. The fear was a smell in his nose, a stench like sewerage. He thought of the first bite and the quickening pulse, the adrenaline coursing through veins in a body primed with terror. It thinned the blood, quickened the pulse, and seemed to warm the flesh in its eagerness to leap from body to lips and on down into him, to be part of him. Then the pulse would slow and the heartbeat fade and the body would be meat, like a cow or sheep.

Always fading, that was the trouble. They were always so tantalisingly, achingly close to sating his ravening hunger without quite filling the hole he always felt at the core of him. He had tried many ways to fill that space but it remained. He had to admit, of all the things he'd tried, this was the very sweetest. To have them and to hold them as close as only their mothers could. To devour a living vessel and truly become one with another soul. Sometimes he thought he would take the entire world into himself and be them all.

As he sat, he cast his mind back to the others, other meals. He remembered each face like they were his own. He remembered each town and city he visited and dined. Some he remembered fondly, others were like nightmares. There had been a few times when he had almost been caught because of some passerby or lucky beat cop; times when a drunk derelict might have stumbled upon him during the act of abduction, or worse, as he ate.

38

He remembered the first time he had tasted human meat; such a revelation could not be readily forgotten. A man had thrown a punch at him in a bar, a fight had ensued and somehow the man got him in a tight bear hug. Without any other means of escape, Jack sank his teeth into the man's cheek and tore viciously at the meat until a good chunk came away in his mouth. The man let go of his hold and clamped a hand to the hole in his face. Coltraine fell to the floor but got to his feet quickly.

Why he hadn't just spit the meat out once the man had let him go, he would never know. He just hadn't. The blood mingled with the meat was pleasurable to his tongue, if a little nicotine tinged. He chewed down and swallowed and his stomach rejoiced at the sensation of the morsel. The man who had attacked him had watched this first with revulsion, then horror. He backed up, falling over a chair in his eagerness for escape. Without pause for breath, he skittered away from Coltraine on his hands and feet; bulging eyes fixed on the madman with blood that was not his own running over smiling lips and down his chin. That had been his first, but by no means his sweetest.

That first encounter had given him strength. He remembered looking at his reflection in the mirror and not recognising the face that stared back at him through the scarlet mask of someone else's blood. This was the apex predator that lurked within him. No, he was not crazed like a rabid dog. The tearing out of the man's cheek was an instinctive response, but he could be much more calculated and cold. He could be smart and dine on human flesh. He could control mankind and they would become his delicatessen. That day, his reflection persuaded him to become a connoisseur of the forbidden meat. The old, the young, the males and females would all find their way to his table and he would honour every meal.

He thought back to his past in the hope of tricking his stomach into accepting the pig as edible, but he failed. After his first taste of human flesh, how could he stomach such offal?

As he sat there munching on a different but no more appetising sandwich that evening, sixteen hours after dumping the girl's body, there was still no word. The girl was "missing, presumed alive" not dead. Good. He might get a couple more good meals yet if the cops were this slow.

****

"Okay, I think we're set," Tommy announced, setting his spade to one side and mopping his brow with his grimed shirt. The drinks were a bad idea. It had taken far more effort than they'd imagined to dig out the cold earth which lay atop Jeffrey's casket. Tommy had freaked out a little, fearing they would never get everything prepared in time. Timing, of course is everything with these things and they didn't want to get caught half way through their endeavour.

It had been Tommy's idea to attempt the working. He had been heartbroken when he had been told of the accident.

He and Jeffrey had grown up together and they'd had a bond. They had been neighbours, or as close to being neighbours as farmers ever got, until Tommy's dad had sold up and moved his family into town. Their mothers had sipped iced tea together on hot summer afternoons while the boys ran riot in the fields.

They had also lost brothers together, both killed in the army far too young. It had drawn the two younger boys close, forged an almost brotherly bond between them.

Chloe had taken the news hard, too. She had also known Jeffrey a long time and had hung around the farm as a young child, laughing at the two boys' antics. She and Jeffrey had grown a little closer over the past few months though and their friendship had turned to something more.

It hadn't taken long for Tommy to reach into his books and find a remedy for their collective pain. Of course, the girls had agreed; they always had. Chloe was always ready to follow the boys' lead, whatever the outcome, and when Jade came to town and joined their group, she fell right in line. So Tommy had taken the blade to first his flesh and then the girls' and carved into them, icons of power and protection. Acquiring the necessary ingredients hadn't proved difficult, either. Cows' blood was easy to come by as were chickens.

So here they all stood now at the foot of Jeffrey's grave. Tommy stripped his shirt off and then poured the blood around the edge of the pit, then inside. He then grabbed the chicken and, chanting the words from his grimoire, he slaughtered it with his silver blade and threw its still fluttering body into the grave, too.

Chloe and Jade joined hands with him and the ritual itself began. In minutes or hours or perhaps even days, they would find out, finally, if they were witches or wasters.

****

Jeffrey watched as his friends chanted the incantation together. He couldn't believe the lengths that their grief had driven them to. They had practiced some minor workings with him, of course they had: the Ouija and tarot. But this was a whole other order of madness. Now that he had seen the sacrifice and the blood, the marks on Tommy's skin, he knew what they were doing. No parlour trick this. This was Necromancy!

No sooner had he reached the realisation, he began to feel the effects of their work. Jeffrey had never been completely certain that there was any magic in the world, never been totally convinced that the spirits had really spoken through the Ouija. Now he had been given the proof that spirits were a reality. Now here was the proof that magic was indeed a reality also.

Jeffrey began to feel pain, excruciating pain where his living body had been struck by the truck. He sank to his knees under the weight of such suffering. Is this what death had kept from him? If so, then oblivion was the kindest of hosts. Through tear-blurred eyes, he watched his friends in magical ecstasies now; rocking backward and forward to the rhythm of their chanting. It was unbearable to watch their complete surrender to whatever power was aiding them, almost as painful as his physical hurt. He looked away, doing his level best to endure the agonies being inflicted upon him by his friends' kindness.

Then, the final horror. Suddenly a wind sprang up from nowhere. The earth oozed and bubbled like lava, working in tandem with the wind to push him and buffet him, and all the time forcing him backward; inexorably back into the midst of his friends. He wrestled desperately with his instincts to run; even in death the survival instinct was ingrained. He needed to escape, to be away from this place of pain, and recover. He had to tell his friends that what they were doing was wrong, against all that was natural. The wind pushed him harder, debris whipping into him, scything through the scant substance of him. He so wanted to shout, to yell into his friends' ears to stop ... to scream.

He struggled against the pain, trying to resist whatever it was that was turning earth and air against him. He didn't want to enter the circle. Once he knew a time when that circle would have meant comfort and warmth. Not now, not this night. He knew what was there; he knew that it would hurt ... a lot.

****

The world knows magic. It recognises power and will react accordingly. There are stains left behind where workings are performed if those looking know the signs to look out for. Small animals know to steer clear of these places, spirits do not tread there out of a certain fear that they may never leave again. That night Tommy, Chloe, and Jade were making a big, dark stain right there in the graveyard.

Tommy could feel it as he chanted the incantation over and over. There were cold, invisible fingers running up and down his spine. He felt it like static before a lightning storm. He knew the girls felt it too as their grip on his hand grew ever tighter, clammier.

He felt the sigils carved into his arms and torso burning and, sure enough, they were indeed glowing red. It hurt far more than carving them had but his excitement far outweighed the pain. As the burning intensified so Tommy's voice grew louder, stronger in the certainty of their success. He smiled as the cold fingers extended their reach up to his skull and down to his groin. He knew the girls felt it too by their gasps of delight as the assault on their senses intensified, sending each of them into paroxysms of delight and desire.

As the incantation came to its third or fourth climax, so did they. As one their bowels voided and sexual juices were loosed and spurted onto the earth. Silken juices trickled down smooth, pale thighs and sank into the ground which, in its turn, drank it down with a hunger. Just how they had ended up naked none of them could tell, but naked they were. No one had said that such magic was so intense, but it was. It was far too much for them. The absolute bombardment of sensation overloaded their synapses and they fell as one. They collapsed–and Jeffrey knocked.

****

Unknown to Tommy and the girls, they were being watched. Unseen eyes saw their every move and understood the business they were about. The apparition smiled from the shadows, knowing what the significance of this moment meant. A working of this magnitude was almost as significant as its own undertaking. How apt.

The dark eyes watched as the children collapsed, almost losing its own gourde even standing at the edge of the cyclone of power which radiated from the grave. Then the sound of knocking rose from the grave, carrying over on the light breeze which passed through the graveyard. That was when the apparition departed, knowing that it was safe to do what he was planning on doing; the things he had already done, if he were being honest.

He knew what they were doing because he had studied the very arts that these mere children were practicing at this moment. He had been left feeling empty by his researches into those realms but he remained a soul wrapped up in darkness; it was just that the darkness wreathed around him was of his own creation.

With a last glance behind him, Jack Coltraine walked from the chapel grounds a lot more confident than he had been before he stumbled onto this scene.

Poor Jeffrey

Life hurt. It was a lesson he had learned as a youngster when he had fallen from a tree in the back yard and broken his collarbone, then again when Penny Hooper had dumped him in favour of Brett Watling. Life hurt in a thousand different ways and more. Resurrection was worse. Being wrenched from the afterlife and locked back in his prison of dead matter and broken bones hurt like crazy. It was dark; it was uncomfortable in his velvet-lined casket. It hurt because he remembered what death felt like. He remembered the absolute freedom of his former state; the warmth, the peace. Compared to death, this was purgatory.

He kicked out with violence. The pain in his arm and chest erupted blindingly but he kicked again, then yet again. His fury burned brighter than the pain as he kicked harder and harder, throwing himself against the sides of his box. Too soon he would realise the full price of his rebirth, he would get around to thinking, but for now rage was enough to fuel him. He kicked once more with such venom he was sure the casket would explode. It didn't. But now he could hear screaming.

****

Tommy whooped and hollered around the graveside as the casket danced around in the ground. Jade stared down over the lip of the pit, a grin etched across her features. "We did

46

it," she breathed, over and over like a mantra.

Chloe was silent for a second. Wide eyed, her head shaking as if to deny her part in this act. And then she screamed. She looked down at her naked body, at the sigils which still glowed across the pale skin of her arms and stomach. She bent and grabbed her clothes, suddenly feeling the need to cover her modesty, all the while shrieking. This was just not possible. The dead could not rise. And yet the casket continued to rattle around in its hole.

"Will someone get me the hell outta here?" Jeffrey's voice was muffled by the wood but it was undoubtedly him and that was what broke Chloe's tenuous hold on her sanity. She turned and ran away, wanting to put as much distance between herself and the scene of her crime against nature, but no distance seemed far enough at that moment; neither the town limits, nor the state line. The world knew what she had done. She felt the ground recoil beneath her feet with every step she took, but still she ran because she could do nothing else.

Tommy and Jade were too preoccupied by the casket and Jeffrey's demands to be set free to notice Chloe's retreat. At the first sound of Jeffrey's voice, Tommy had dropped into the hole and set about trying to break the casket open with a crowbar. After a second or two, Jade dropped into the hole beside him and lent a hand and pushed on the bar with Tommy. A second later the upper portion of the lid flew open, smashing into the wall of the grave and there he was, dead but walking once more. Poor Jeffrey returned to them.

Jeffrey moved suddenly, leaping out of the box to his feet in one fluid motion and grabbing Tommy by the throat. The pain, fear, and rage combined to make him cruel and he punched Tommy in the stomach. "Do you know what you've done to me?" he screamed into Tommy's face.

"We brought you back, dude!" Tommy gasped. "Like fucking Lazarus, bro. I thought you'd be happy."

"Happy? I was dead! How do I explain this, Tom? And it hurts. I'm hurting from being hit by a truck. Did you even stop to think about that?" Jeffrey shouted into his friend's face. His temper abated slightly, though, and he released his grip on his throat.

"But you'll fix. It won't be forever," Tommy reasoned.

"I won't fix. I'm dead here, shitwit!" Jeffrey hissed.

"You're not dead, Jeff. You're back, you're here."

"Feel," cried Jeffrey, holding out his wrist. "No pulse!"

"That. Can't. Be." Tommy hissed, his certainty tested. "It worked like it said."

"Yes it did, Tommy, but you only read what you wanted to read. What's dead is dead, dude."

"But ... it said–"

"Did it say you'd shit on the floor and jizz on your toes?"

"No, but ... how did you know that?" Tommy blushed.

"It doesn't matter ... nothing does now." Jeffrey sighed, turned, and hauled himself out of the grave.

"Where're you going?" Tommy called after him.

"I don't know. Somewhere I'm not gonna freak anybody out in the morning?" he replied. He didn't look back as he limped away.

"You should thank me!" Tommy yelled, his bravado returning.

There was no reply.

****

He liked to walk late at night when the town slept and he had the streets to himself, so quiet he could imagine himself the sole survivor of some Armageddon. The silence seemed to fold around him like a blanket and his thoughts came clearer than they ever could during the day. He had to concentrate hard on his many pretensions then, lest they all come crashing down. Standing in the sunlight he was the embodiment of someone else; Jack Coltraine today, who knew who else he would be in a week. At night he could be himself and it felt good. Free.

He liked the town. Old Jack had fallen right in with the pace of things. It hadn't taken long to mingle with the other travelers who worked the land; it was a familiar enough role. The townsfolk were pleasant enough and just the right side of ignorant for him to feel safe without wanting to murder every stupid one of them. He hated stupidity.

Cal Denver, the creature behind Jack's eyes, was a highly intelligent man. He was quietly calculating and loved to manipulate the simple minded. He loved the game he was playing, evading the law. Making even the smartest of them appear slow witted. Most of all though, he just loved the taste of flesh.

He was headed home and wondering about the mute girl, wondering how long it would be until her remains were discovered; calculating how long he might be able to stay and how many more meals he might find. He hoped for many. The flames of his hope flared as he neared what passed for his home.

He was about to leave the road and cut across the field to his right when the girl bolted out of the trees on the opposite side. She ran right into him, eyes wide and tears streaming down her cheeks. Instinctively, he wrapped his arms around her as she crumpled, trembling against him. He snapped himself into Coltraine's thought processes and held her a little tighter. "What's wrong, Little Miss? What happened?" he soothed in Coltraine's country hick drone. The girl tried to reply, but her grief strangled her words in her throat. And so, uttering kindly words into her hair, he led her across the field to the tumble-down farmhouse for a cup of tea or some brandy. Perhaps even a small bite to eat.

****

"What an ungrateful shit!" hissed Tommy for the twentieth time. "How could he just go at me? Did you see him?"

"I saw, Tommy. He's just in shock, that's all. We did just let him out of his grave," Jade soothed, rubbing his arm.

"Well, screw him. You hear? Fucking. Screw. Him." Tommy snarled and downed more liquor.

50

It had been over an hour since Jeffrey had left them. Now here they were, back in the woods drinking and smoking a joint like normal. Like nothing had happened.

They'd just dressed and gone back to normality. Tommy's rage had not subsided a bit in that time, he just continued to rail against the unfairness of the situation. Jeffrey should be with them, celebrating. He should be thankful, grateful. And where the hell had Chloe got to? Jade had tried to placate him, to quiet his rage, but to no avail. The boy was far too consumed by his feeling of injustice at the way Jeffrey had treated him, after the efforts they'd gone to. Jade couldn't seem to get through to him.

Not yet.

Jade had seen Jeffrey clearly, not blinded by fear or rage. She never had the same connection as the others had. She hadn't grown up with them so she was not so blind to the changes that had been wrought on Jeffrey by their working. As he had pushed past her to get to Tommy, she had seen it. What Jeffrey had said was true. He was not truly living. Something in his eyes, his scent, the way he had moved. Something had gone awry in the working, but what was it? She couldn't know the answers, not yet, but she would find them. In the meantime, she had to console Tommy or fear for his sanity. Her own was hanging on only by a thread. Gently she went over to Tommy and held him tight to her. "It's gonna be ok, Tom. We'll figure this out," she whispered.

"You promise?" he asked, sounding like the little boy he truly was.

"I do," she assured him with more certainty than she felt.

****

Chloe had always had a morbid curiosity. No one knew where it had come from but it had always been a part of her. It was what had compelled her to take part in Tommy's ritual. Morbid curiosity. It was why she was hanging around now if she were honest, watching the steady rise and fall of the chest. It had surprised her how much the body could endure to prolong life, even the lie of life. She had died many moments ago yet her lungs still filled and emptied, filled and emptied, at least as much as her ragged and torn windpipe would allow. The wounds inflicted upon her were heinous; she could barely stand to look further down her body than her face. At least that was intact, she thought.

He had been nice, at least at first. He had held her tight and consoled her, been patient as she had sobbed and stuttered. Once she regained her composure, he handed her a large measure of brandy and apologized for the squalid state of the home into which he'd invited her.

He was charming, even when he had bitten her and kept on biting. He was much too strong to fight off and she was ditzy from drink; from the brandy and all the other drinks she'd downed earlier in the evening. He had no trouble with his meal at all. If she were not so disgusted it might even have been pleasurable, not pleasant perhaps, but at least understandable. "I'll keep you inside me, nice and safe. Part of me," he said over and over as her blood ran down his chin. It was almost sweet, the way he spoke. If he hadn't been chewing on her flesh.

Then her perspective had changed. She was no longer watching from behind her eyes but off to one side, totally detached. That was when her morbid curiosity had kicked in. She could have turned and fled, or at least averted her gaze, but there was something strangely hypnotic about the sight. That and the fact he could no more harm her now than he could vomit her torn pieces back into life. He chose each bite carefully; treating her body reverentially, almost lovingly. But it was afterward that her curiosity was truly piqued, when he had eaten his fill and began to clean up the mess; wiping the blood from his chin and ministering to her body respectfully, shrouding her body in a blanket.

He wept the whole time, tears streaking his cheeks as he carried her remains to his car; as he scrubbed the blood from the stone floor of the house; as he washed the blood from his hands and face. He grieved.

Now, she stood by the stream in the woods she'd walked through so often and watched her body expire. Letting go its pretence of life, her husk breathed its last. Show over.

****

Jade walked home alone, casting her mind over the events that had brought her to where she stood at this moment. Not just the raising of Jeffrey, which was horrific enough if she thought too long about it, but what had come before. Maybe even the things that had happened to bring her to the town in the first place.

Her father was in big business and was highly successful; it made her mother a lady of leisure. She had lived in the city, gone to school, and tried to be the normal girl. That was impossible, of course. Had she attended a boarding school or one of the private schools, she might have fit in better among the children of her father's associates. That wasn't how her parents saw things though. So she was the daughter of a ridiculously wealthy man, attending a ghetto school. Her mother told her it was so that she would appreciate her fortune when she one day inherited the family money.

Jade had kicked against her parents and started embracing her place in the ghetto, and not among the good kids trying to find a way out. She became a gangster, of sorts. She carried a gun, took drugs, and drank often. She had spent a few nights in the jail, her father refusing to bring her home until she had experienced the holding cells for a time. Even that hadn't worked, so her father bought the little house in this little town.

Jeffrey Kinsey had been the first to say hi, to offer a friendly hand. She roundly ignored it as she ignored every other showing of kindness she was offered. Other kids in the school thought her snobbish, especially when they discovered who her parents were. All but Jeffrey, Chloe, and Tommy, that is.

Pretty soon she relented and began hanging out with

them, and soon after that she grew to love them and relax around them. It was she who had introduced Tommy, crazy, impetuous Tommy, to the Ouija and the tarot. It was she who had rolled them their first joints. In turn, they showed her a real sense of friendship and togetherness. It was a feeling she had never known, so used to suspicion and double talk as she was. These were the first people she had ever met who had no agenda. She liked that.

Now, she was a different girl to the one who had moved into town, but her problems had suddenly grown. What had begun as a little immature fun in the name of grief had turned to something far more. She felt the taint of it deep within her; like a poison it burned at the back of her throat, but it also seemed to empower her. She couldn't quite name the feeling she was experiencing, but she would endeavour to find a way to convey it. How else would she know if Tommy and Chloe had felt the same things?

In the woods she had promised Tommy that she would fix everything, that she would figure it out, and as she walked home that's exactly what she resolved to do. To fix things.

****

His anger soon evaporated into remorse. Jeffrey had never been one for rages and he had regretted his outburst almost as soon as he left the graveyard. He couldn't turn at his friend's call though. He needed time to think all this through.

Dying and getting used to being dead had been a tough

notion once, but he'd been getting there. This was terrible, this unlife he had been thrust into. It hurt so much, but how could he blame his friends for what they had done? Wouldn't he have wanted to do the same had one of them died and he lived? Of course he would.

Tomorrow he would find Tommy and the girls, talk it out and figure how they could put all this right. His life was wrong, that much was plain to him.

What to do in the meantime though? He couldn't walk around until daybreak and certainly couldn't be seen around town. He wandered a while longer. Though his bones ached and pained him where they were badly reset, he had to walk. He was trying to put his thoughts in some semblance of order. When the pain became too much and he felt like he could walk no more, he turned for home, to the farm on which he'd grown up. He couldn't risk his mother seeing him, not yet, but his father would be able to handle the shock ... perhaps. He had to take the risk though. If not home then where could he go?

So he went home, letting himself into the house with the spare key that was always kept under the porch steps.

There he was when his father rose, his heavy feet thudding across the landing to the bathroom and the pause as he emptied his bladder and then washed. Jeffrey listened to the steps as they went back to the bedroom, the creak of the bedsprings as his father sat to put his socks on; then thudding again as he descended the stairs and went to the kitchen for his first cup of coffee of the day. Those familiar sounds, the sounds he'd woken to every morning of his life. It sounded comforting to Jeffrey and a little mournful to his ear this morning.

Tyrone Kinsey liked to think that he was a reasonable man, a rational man. He wasn't particularly religious, but he always attended church during all the premium festivals. He held no strong political views but was always in line at the polling booths come Election Day to put his mark by a name on the slip and post it in the anonymous little box. For all he cared the results could be a dupe. He didn't drink overmuch nor take drugs, he didn't have the time for those kinds of pursuits, but he was generally accepting of how the rest of the world went about its business. Just as long as his cows gave milk and his crops grew plentiful he was a content man. But this morning, the morning after burying his second son, Tyrone Kinsey was faced with the most unreasonable sight he could dare to imagine. The only response his trembling, dry lips could muster was "Good God in heaven help me," as his youngest son rose to greet him.

"Dad ..." Jeffrey began.

"Don't you talk to me like you know me, you demon motherfucker. How dare you!" Tyrone growled, his mind a reeling mess.

"Dad, it's me."

"No!" Tyrone exclaimed, head shaking his denial. "No. My son is dead and in his grave. I don't know what you are, but you're not my boy."

"It's me, Dad, I promise." Jeffrey sighed, sinking back

into his chair. "Just sit down and I can explain."

Tyrone took a step forward with hands balled tightly into fists at his side, as if he might try to beat this hellspawn sitting at his dinner table in a fight. Yet when his eyes met those of the apparition, his shoulders sagged and he crumpled as if he had been punched himself. Sudden realisation and then belief flooded his eyes. "Jeff?" he asked uncertainly.

"Yes, Dad, it's me," came the reply.

"You're alive. You're home!" Tyrone cried, tears streaming down his face. He embraced his son tightly, but quickly released him when Jeffrey cried out in pain.

"I'm not alive, I don't think, but I am home."

"What do you mean by that?" Tyrone asked, eyebrow raised.

Jeffrey explained in the loosest terms he could what had happened to him. He left his friends out of the tale he told and his father didn't question it even though the boy knew that Tyrone was not a stupid man and would see right through the deceit. He just sat and listened to the boy. What else could he do? When his story was finished, Tyrone just sighed. "So what do we do, son?"

"I don't know, Dad. I'm sorry."

"You've got nothing to be sorry for. You didn't ask for this to happen," Tyrone said, incredulous. "Now, I'm your dad and we're going to figure this out. I don't know how right now, but we will. Now, you go on up to your room and rest a while. Keep the curtains closed. I'll go speak to your mother in a bit and then we'll work it all out."

He watched his son leave the room after exchanging an embrace, tears stinging his eyes. Tyrone might have sat at the table for an hour or all the morning, but he just sat and wept, trying to figure out what to say to his wife. He remembered the pain and the grief in her eyes, the look on his son's dead face as he lay in his casket. Now he was returned to them. Did it matter how? Apparently it did. In his heart it mattered because the tears wouldn't stop falling.

****

Father Terence Cade had landed the job of his dreams, a vicarage in a small town where nothing would ever happen. He enjoyed the predictable round of christenings, marriages, and funerals that would be his stable along with the usual Sunday sermons. It wasn't a troubled neighbourhood; it was a township of good old guys and gals from the olden days. He had worked in missions and churches in cities the length and breadth of the country, he had spoken in great depth on the subject of the inner city. In the good sheriff he sensed an awkward kind of kinship through their respective histories. In all, it was a perfect semi-retirement.

That morning, like every morning, he took a walk around the chapel grounds with his dog, Exodus. He enjoyed the clean morning air, before the farmers got into their tractors and trucks and started mussing the air up with diesel fumes. In the city that stink was all pervasive and ever present, here in the country it was all but gone in the wee hours and it remained gone until a couple of hours after sunrise. Early morning was the time that Father Cade enjoyed most, with his dog and the silence of the morning.

For such a small chapel, the graveyard was large, filled with generations of townspeople and their grandfathers. It took him almost an hour to reach the south-eastern end where the new burials were. He liked to see the new graves, all mounted up with fresh flowers, a shining marble tombstone standing erect at its head. The sight filled him with a huge sense of pride. Not like the broken and vandalised tributes that stood in his former ward. Those filled him with sadness and dread for a world that could honour nothing, not even its dead.

He came to within a few feet of Jeffrey Kinsey's grave, hoping to stop a while to read some of the cards that were attached like leaves to the flower arrangements. As he came abreast his heart began to beat double time in his chest. The grave was open; all the dirt that had been thrown on top of the coffin had been shoveled out. He peered over the lip of the hole and saw to his horror that the coffin was open.

The creeping daylight was kind and kept the true horror of what lay within from the preacher's eyes, but still the sight of the open and robbed out grave set him to retreat. What order of madness was this, which in this quiet corner a person would steal a corpse?

He didn't stop running until he made the house and made a hurried call to the sheriff. This crime could not be allowed to stand, in the name of any god.

****

Tommy's indignation did not subside. It only intensified with isolation. Since Jade had left him he had stewed in his anger and feelings of injustice. He washed his grimed clothes and silently raged at the unfairness of it all. Had he not laid himself on the line? Had he not offered his soul, and the souls of his friends, for the working? It had been a success, Jeffrey was alive, and yet everything had still turned sour. The passage of time, however short, was proving the wrongness of his actions, but he had closed his eyes to that. He had carved the sigils in his flesh and offered up blood. What more had to be done? Was it Tommy's mistake that Jeffrey had returned incomplete? Had the working been compromised?

He lay on his bed sweating as the sun rose, sorting through the events of the night and the mistakes he had made even after the event. All might be well if the girls kept quiet. Yes, they had left the grave open and they should have cleared up their paraphernalia that could all be traced back to him, but if Jeffrey kept out of sight and the girls kept calm then all didn't have to be lost. There would still be some good come out of this; he was determined that there would. He would not put his soul on the line and have what he'd worked so hard to achieve go to corruption in his grasp.

How could Tommy know what had befallen Chloe? How was he to know the events that had been set in motion as a result of his grief?

Even as he lay and pondered his ponderings, Jade was

making plans of her own. Plans which involved the getting and the using of power.

Chloe was already the victim of another madman's design. But how could Tommy know this? How could he know that creatures even darker than himself lived in his safe corner of the world? True monsters exist only in dreams, after all.

****

"That's what I said, Sheriff. The body, grave, and casket were all as they ought to be when I left last night. Now ... this!" exclaimed Father Cade, gesturing toward the open grave. His eyes had a wild expression, almost deranged with outrage. The good Father needed to be handled carefully and so the sheriff nodded at one of his deputies. Jayne Freese came over and took the priest by the arm, leading him away from the graveside. And so began the strangest few days that Klimpt Davies had ever, or would ever, have to live through. He had lived in the town for over twenty years and been sheriff for fifteen. In all that time he'd needed to do little more than issue a traffic violation in pursuit of justice. Now this?

He had looked into the hole and seen no body, just an open casket. He wasn't prepared for this, not in the slightest. Bodysnatching? Wasn't that a thing of the past? He stood over the grave, hands on hips and head shaking in utter disbelief. "Why would anyone steal a corpse?" he asked no one in particular and received only blank stares by way of reply.

He looked again into the empty grave and recoiled at the sight at the bottom of the grave. Was that a chicken lying where the head of the corpse should've been? Was that blood spatter on the casket? It was, and more blood on the grass at his feet. He turned and looked hard at his deputy, Josh Barrett. "Get on the phone. We need some kinda specialist down here," he said grimly.

"What kinda specialist do we need, sir?" Barrett asked.

"I don't fucking know. Someone who knows about blood and DNA. There's blood all over here!"

"Yes, sir," Barrett said. "A pathologist then?"

"If you say so, fucking smart ass," snapped Davies. He was cranky and impatient, too many years in the force under his belt. He had taken the transfer to the town simply because of its quietude; he was too old and tired for this kind of weirdness. Crimes like these were for hungry city boys or up and coming agency guys, not relics like him. His wife had been right only days before–he should have retired.

Yet as events were to unfold, he would realise that there were far stranger things abroad in his district and soon he would know them by name.

****

Jeffrey preferred death. It was hot within the confines of his body; it was cloying. It was a prison of filth, dead matter, and oozing fluids. Compared with his existence as a spirit, it was hell. In fact, he thought, all those who had written at any great length about Hades as a place of flame and pain had probably died and been reborn. Hell was life for him now. His heart didn't beat, his blood was still in his veins and it felt unnatural. He tried to sleep, but he was too uncomfortable inside his own skin. Wrong. It was all so wrong.

After an age, or only a scant few moments later, he heard his father's heavy step on the stairs and then his parents' bedroom door creaked open. He heard his father's voice as a low rumble through the wall, barely audible. Then he heard his mother scream and running footsteps across the landing. Less than a heartbeat later she was there, sobbing into his hair and drowning him in kisses. After a few moments of such claustrophobia, he almost screamed but made himself relax, breathe. Then he settled into the familiar, comforting embrace of his mother.

****

"Look, you stupid shit. What's gonna happen is that my boys are gonna start searching the woods and we're gonna help find the girl. There ain't nothin' you can do to stop it. I have the men. I have the resources. You ain't got shit!" Frank Fielding growled down the line.

"It's not a case of ..." came the strained voice in reply.

"Look, Sheriff. I'm doing this. Like it or not." Fielding growled.

"Well, just don't get in the way of my boys, Frank." The sheriff sighed.

"Good. Now you're seeing sense. I'll see you on my land tomorrow."

He slammed the phone down and gulped the last of the drink he'd poured himself mid call. He had a suspicion that Davies would oppose his plans and so he had, giving the spiel about evidence and care in the search. In the end, there was little the Sheriff Davies could do to stop him. If Frank Fielding wanted to do something around the place, it happened.

The disappearance of the little girl from the town park had hit Fielding hard. It showed him that his home wasn't the safe haven that it once was; that what his forebears had attempted to build was turning to manure, just like every other place in the country and throughout the world. It wasn't the vision that Fielding had for the place, either. One day his son or daughters would return home to run the family business and they would want to live the way he had, surely. He had to protect that bubble of perfection. The only way to do that was to join the search and at least attempt to catch the person responsible. It was his duty as the single strongest pillar of the community.

Now he sat in his study with the newspaper in front of him. The picture of the little mute girl stared up at him, as it had done for several days now. Had his wife been alive it may not have consumed him so totally, but he had no way of diverting his attention from his purpose. When Hattie had been alive, she had soothed him out of these moods of preoccupation. She would joke about it and he would remove himself to the land of people, TVs, and rumour. No longer though. Now he sat up until the early hours and obsessed over details, options, and paths of influence. Here he saw only two options: get out of town and live by the sea, turn his back on the whole business or step up in a way that no one else seemed able.

As was Fielding's wont, he chose the latter. He picked up the telephone and began dialling numbers, calling in favours and asking for a few of his own.

****

Tyrone Kinsey walked out into the fields, not even bothering to pretend that he was working. He sat with his back to the front wheel of his truck, parked in one of the fields furthest away from the house. He needed time and space to think. The events this early morning were too much even for him to digest. He was a practical man, a man who believed in the natural order. He was a farmer and he wasn't superstitious, but what he had seen in his kitchen even he would describe as ungodly. Regardless of the shape this creature had taken, it couldn't be his son. It couldn't be the boy he had watched grow, taken into the fields and played games with. His entire body bristled with contradictions and doubts.

Yet despite his doubt, he had allowed it to stay in his home and play out its pretence. He had allowed his wife to accept it as her son, to embrace it and to cry into its hair. Perhaps that was more a kindness to his wife, a salve to the hurt that had consumed her so completely after her son's death. He couldn't deny her a moment with the apparition that, however grotesque the thought, might be their offspring.

Even now he didn't truly understand what it was he had spoken to or how to deal with it. The thing knew him, had spoken with his boy's voice so perfectly. When he looked into the boy's eyes, it was so undoubtedly his son staring back at him. Could there be a counterfeit so close to its template?

Usually the fields calmed him, now the entire world seemed out of kilter like someone had crept upon the earth during the night and knocked it askew. He needed time, he needed quiet, but the bees were so damned loud as they went about their morning business.

He had called all his farm hands and made sure they didn't go to the house. The events of the past week had made a story of Marie being unable to stand people tramping through the house believable. He felt bad about lying to these men but he had no choice. He needed a little time to figure things out, to speak with the thing that was his son. Then he would know what he had to do.

If only he could think!

****

Jade couldn't sleep; she was too wired from last night's events. It had changed everything for her. New dreams, new possibilities had opened up to her. She could feel power moving, right at the core of her. She had kept it a secret from Tommy; wrapped up as he was in his own petty grievances he wouldn't have been interested in any of her revelations. She might never tell him, or anyone else. That way, it was hers and hers alone. That sounded good.

She vaguely remembered the girl that she'd been before she'd hooked up with Tommy and the others. She'd been the new girl in town, daughter of a rich father who never showed his face in town. She was a big city girl and hated everything about the town; she was worldlier than the other kids and a good number of the adults there. It had all been so ordinary, so grey. Until the night she'd gone to the woods with the others.

There she had found her crowd and together they had experimented with drugs and magic in a way that she never could have done in the city, and they had followed her just for the sheer fun of it. Where last night it had seemed like a kindness, now it seemed absurd, naïve. Now she had a revelation, some kind of treasure bestowed on her for the things that she had done and if the others didn't realise that, then more fool them. She reveled in it. She touched the skin of her arms, just for the frisson of the touch, feeling as it did like a new skin.

She had made a promise to fix things, and that felt totally possible. In her mind it was a piffling thing. All she needed to do was talk to Tommy, and all would be repaired. If he did as she asked.

****

"I haven't cried. I should be sad."

That was Chloe's thought as she watched her parents sleep. She stood in the corner watching the gentle rise and fall of the sheets; she even enjoyed the sounds of her father's snoring. She wouldn't stay much longer. Dawn was breaking and she didn't want to see her parents panic at her absence and eventual grief when her remains were uncovered; that would be unbearable. Where she would go was an issue for later. For now, she was putting her thoughts in order.

She had made a stupid mistake. She had done exactly what she had admonished a thousand ditzy blondes for doing in a thousand horror flicks. She remembered all the times she had shouted at the TV screen, "Why run? Stay with the group. The killer's out there ... dolt." And yet she had done that very same thing; run into the arms of her killer. It was almost comical.

She thought about Tommy and Jade, about what had led her to her undoing. She had screamed and run, of course she had. Had she thought for a moment that their attempt at resurrection would work, she would never have gone to the graveyard. Yet there she had gone. She could blame no one but herself for her death.

She remembered school and the group she found herself in. Tommy and Jeffrey had been ever present in her life; they were the farm kids that the town kids would never accept into their own circles. Jade had arrived later but she was no less a part of the group, she was an outsider, too. And so they had drawn tight to each other through the bad times and the good. Through the triumphs in school to the lows of the deaths of Tommy's and Jeffrey's brothers. All those things had bonded them.

Death had surprised her. There was no chorus of angels or tunnels of white light, just a slight jolt and a sudden shift of perception. No pain or panic, no great revelation, just a detached continuance. She tingled all over her body, like a mild alcohol buzz, which was quite pleasant.

Things could be much, much worse, she thought. If this was the state that Jeffrey had found himself in then she was sorry for what she had helped to do to him. She was sorry anyway. Perhaps that was why she wasn't being punished; perhaps this was her punishment. Maybe there was no punisher.

She put her musing aside as her mother stirred and rolled over in her sleep. She gestured at something in her dreams, then muttered lightly. "I love you, Mama." Chloe breathed.

"I love you too, honey," her mother murmured absently.

****

Dr. Prentzler was an odious little man who Sheriff Davies hated with a passion. He was the kind of man who reveled in his own intelligence, especially those less learned than he. The man spoke like he was lecturing students; Davies had once overheard him ordering coffee in the same manner and assumed it was the man's approximation of a social tone.

He was sat opposite him now, fingertips pushed together to make a pyramid of his hands, his pontification on DNA into its twentieth minute. The blood in the grave was inhuman, the doctor assured him; proteins and factors in the plasma indicating it to be bovine. And on, and on. One phrase caught his attention among the jargon and the medical mumbo jumbo, however. That phrase sent cold shivers down his spine and turned his legs to water. The doctor had apparently moved on from DNA and medicine, now it was the history of magic. The chicken, the blood; all pointed to the use of dark magic. Devil worship. Davies looked at Prentzler through narrowed eyes, searching with suspicion. Then he pulled out two glasses and a bottle of scotch.

"You want a drink, Doc? I definitely need one after that."

"I sense you have little appetite for my words, Sheriff," the doctor said.

"I don't have the appetite for talk of demon worship, Doc. It paints pictures in my mind that I thought I forgot," Davies said grimly.

"From your time in the big smoke, I assume?" Prentzler urged, taking the drink that Davies proffered.

"Yep. And I ain't gonna talk about it, so don't waste your breath. Tell me about this case."

"Well, it isn't simple. What we have is a missing body and some kind of rite done over the grave site. The human body can be used for all sorts of purposes. There are tribes in South America who use parts of the body in rituals and I

71

know of several cases in Europe where the bodies of men were used for some potion or other. Honestly, to give details would be sheer guesswork on my part. The possibilities are almost limitless."

"Gimme your best guess."

"Honestly I wouldn't like to say, not until the body is recovered. I will say this though. Whoever did this was watching the area for burials. Not many people are buried these days; cremation is the far cheaper option."

"So you're saying that whoever did this was local?"

"I'm saying whoever did this was watching the obituaries and looking out for burials. If we assume that the person would see the local press then yes, that person would be local to the area. With the internet as well, I wouldn't rule out cities within say … a hundred miles?"

"A hundred miles!" exclaimed the sheriff. "Then we won't ever find Kinsey's body."

"It would be doubtful, but that is your job–not mine, Sheriff."

"Yeah, thanks."

"I can only give you the facts as they present themselves. And on that note, I should get back to the hospital," Prentzler said, rising from his chair.

"If anything springs to mind, let me know."

"One thing does occur, as you ask …"

"Go on."

"These disappearances, the little girl in the park … Has it struck you that these could be connected?" asked the doctor.

"It has, but I'm not going down that route, not just yet."
The sheriff groaned; it was a possibility he didn't wish to
contemplate.

"Then I'll leave you to your work," Prentzler said, and left
the room.

****

Ray Valance had three routes he used alternatively. The
routes he had planned to simulate the conditions he would
face in a real race situation. He had driven to Latimer's Creek
once that week already and it had almost defeated him. It
would not do so again. He sat on the edge of the tailgate of
his truck and tied his shoelaces, contemplating the challenges
the terrain would throw up in front of him. With a sigh he
tightened his jaw and set off with his confident stride.

The sweat began to trickle between his shoulder blades
almost as soon as he set off across the fields, through patches
of tall grass and barley. Coming toward the first wooded part
of his route, about twenty minutes in, was a welcome respite
from the glaring sun. He followed the well-trodden path into
the trees but veered off after just a little way in. Off the
beaten track was a secondary way which followed the banks
of a cool, burbling stream. He had spotted a beaver dam
earlier in the week; perhaps today he might be fortunate
enough to spot the architect.

He was wrenched from thoughts of his ambition by his
sudden fall. One moment he was running, his rhythm good,

thinking thoughts of wildlife. The next moment he was tumbling down the shallow side of the river bank. When he came to a halt he sat up gingerly, checking himself for any damage. Assured that his injuries were minor, he looked around and then his gaze fell to the ground beside him.

The scream he let out at the sight made birds flock in panic to the sky, lending their own shrieks to his. He scrabbled away from the shock of red hair, the beatific smile; the hollowed out torso and meatless arms. The sight would burn in his mind until the day he died.

****

That morning, Cal Denver was smiling behind the solemn gaze of Jack Coltraine. The perversity of fate astounded and amused even him. Oh, this would be such a fun day. One to boast about.

He arrived on the field for work to find it a mess of flashing cameras; there at Frank's invitation, much to Sheriff Davies' obvious irritation. The workforce was gathered in a huddle around a map of the country which surrounded the town. Frank Fielding was dividing the areas around the town into quadrants, then dividing the men into parties of five and sending them out to search a quadrant. The boss man wanted to be seen to be a man of action, a pillar of the community. He wanted to be seen to be joining the search and doing everything he could to find the little mute girl.

Votes might depend on his actions here come Election

Day. The cameras flashed as still more pictures were taken. Fielding's solemn face would be on local TV and in the newspapers pretty damn quick. He would stand in the foreground with the sheriff's surly face floating over his shoulder like a threat. Cal could barely suppress a giggle at the sight of it. Oh, but it was perfect, being a part of all this, seeing the thing he had set in motion from the other side; rubbing shoulders with the people who should, and would, soon be searching for him with a murderous rage. Before they headed out to begin the search, they gathered around Fielding as Father Cade prayed for their success and gave thanks for their service. Cal had to suppress a laugh at the man's piousness. It was all so very comic.

Now he sat in a truck with four guys he knew vaguely. He kept quiet, nodding in acknowledgement with their assertions of what they would do to any guy they suspected of "*screwin'
around*" with a little girl. He was working things out, making sure he was safe to be taking the risks that he was taking. He was fitting in, and being one of the guys. It was easy because it was not an act, Jack Coltraine thought in exactly the same way as these men; he was one of them. Jack had been born in a community like this; he had been raised with hicks like these. It was a kind of home away from home.

Cal Denver, on the other hand, so out of place in these types of towns, sat behind Jack Coltraine's eyes and just enjoyed the show.

****

Poor Jeffrey had to listen to his mother lie to the cops when they arrived and the sound was like nails being driven into his heart. She was neither a liar nor a criminal, now he had made her both by his mere presence. Still, he listened to her act. It was only fair that he listened, it was all for his benefit. After a while he heard the cops voices at the front door, then his mother's, thick with emotion as she thanked them for their kindnesses. He heard final condolences being offered, then crunching footsteps outside.

A few seconds later, he heard two doors slam closed and an engine start, recede and disappear. A few beats later and his mother was there again, by his side.

"I'm sorry about that, Mama. You didn't need to do that for me," he said quietly.

"Do what? I didn't do anything wrong." She smiled.

"You lied to the cops, Mama. They can arrest you for that."

"I know that. But I couldn't figure how to tell them the truth; they would've thought I was crazy. And even if I could, you are my son. I don't know how this came to be and, honestly, I don't care. I got you back. I lost your brother and it broke my heart ... losing you, too? That near killed me but you came back to me. That's all that matters right now." She stroked his hand tenderly, her blue eyes swimming in moisture.

"I'm sorry ... it's just ... I'm ... just sorry," Jeffrey stuttered.

"Just nothing. Now you rest. You've been through a lot these last few hours. Leave figuring this out to your dad and me." She smiled.

"You can't, Mom. It can't be figured out, it's … complicated."

"I think I can guess it's complicated, son." She laughed, just a little. "You hungry?"

"I am. A little," Jeffrey lied. He hadn't felt hunger at all since his resurrection.

****

Just as the two cops were driving away from the Kinsey house, unknowing of what sat in the bedroom just feet above them, Eddie Clarke and Brad Collins set out into the field just north of town alongside Carl Hooper and the guy who was working the summer on the Grove, Jack Coltraine, to search for the little girl from town. As all that was going on, Cassie Kenworth picked up the phone and dialled the number for Sheriff Davies' office to report her daughter missing. As she waited for the connection to be made, her husband went to the door in answer to the insistent, officious knocking. At the sight of Sheriff Davies following her husband inside, she dropped the receiver.

"Mrs. Kenworth? I think you oughta take a seat, ma'am," he said, grimly.

A little later and Klimpt Davies was driving back to the crime scene. The call had come in mere moments after

Prentzler had left the office. It had taken the sheriff scant minutes to reach the scene. What he saw was beyond his intellect to describe and he almost lost his gourd at the sight of young Chloe Kenworth, opened up and left for carrion. Now he was returning to the spot, to look around and see what could be seen.

Grimly, he thought of the chances of the younger girl being found alive. This turn of events would surely shorten her odds. In a town like this, the chances of two crazies acting independently of each other were slim. No, the same guy who had taken the little mute girl was the same who had done this act to the young Kenworth girl. Maybe even the same guy who had taken the body of Jeffrey Kinsey. Although he had denied the possibility to the doctor, now he was forced to face the facts that everything that was happening was connected to one culprit. And he must be caught. He narrowed his mind to concentrate on that one fact … the killer must be caught at all costs.

****

Marie Kinsey washed the dishes in her kitchen and set about making sandwiches for herself and her son. She hummed as she buttered the bread and started laying ham and cheese on, ladling spoons of pickle on top. She was almost happy, in a sense.

After the events of the week past, she could be forgiven for overlooking the impossibility of what she was doing; for ignoring the glaringly obvious fact that her dead son was now sitting in his bedroom awaiting his lunch. It didn't matter to her. Jeffrey had come back to her. That was the only fact that she needed at that moment. Anything less would send her into such a dark place she didn't even want to comprehend returning. Not yet.

She thought back to happier times at the little farmhouse, when she had first moved in with Tyrone. He was a kind man, totally devoted to her happiness. He had offered to leave the farm and move to the city with her but she couldn't drag him from the only home he had ever known. Ty, he wouldn't know what to do if he didn't have the fields out back to wander in and tend to. It still made her smile after so many years.

She remembered her boys, one grown so big and muscular, the younger smart and bookish. They were both handsome boys in her eyes and people a mother could be proud of. It had devastated her when her eldest son had died so needlessly, it was more than any mother could bear, to lose a child. Marie had done so twice now. Perhaps the world felt her pain and had chosen to take back the hurt it had done her in taking both of her boys from her. Perhaps even the earth itself couldn't see a woman suffer the loss of two children and had chosen to breathe new life into her youngest boy.

Of course, her rational mind knew that this was not the case but for now it was explanation enough. She went back to making sandwiches and remembered her sons as they once were.

Poor Jeffrey

****

Tommy ignored all his calls the following day and feigned sickness so he could stay away from school. Jade had called a couple of times and Jeffrey's mother once, apparently an invite to go and collect some things of her son's that he might want as a keepsake. The subtext of the message was pretty clear; Jeffrey wanted to see him. That, or Mrs. Kinsey wasn't aware of her son's resurrection. It didn't matter which, he couldn't face seeing Mrs. Kinsey. He just wanted to forget that whole night and its events, but he knew that was never going to happen.

Somewhere around eleven in the morning, there was a knock at the door. He heard his mother answer and call his name a few moments later. When he went to see what she wanted, he saw his mother serving iced tea to two of Sheriff Davies' deputies. As soon as he saw their grim faces he wanted to run but knew it was pointless.

"Tommy!" his mother exclaimed in that sing-song voice that she knew grated on his nerves. "These gentlemen have some news."

"Really? What news?" Tommy asked.

"Well, not so much news. Questions. We think you already know about our news, Tommy," said the burly guy on the left, Deputy Barrett. "You gonna take a seat?"

"I'm fine standing, thanks," Tommy said evenly.

"I want to ask you some questions about your friends, Tommy," Barrett said.

"So … ask," replied Tommy.

"We'd prefer to speak privately," suggested the one on the left. Tommy didn't know him.

"Ain't nothing you can't say in front of my mum," assured Tommy.

"If that's the way you want it. What do you know about Jeffrey Kinsey's corpse going missing last night?" the officer asked.

"Nothing, not until just now," Tommy replied. "Sorry, I didn't catch your name, sir."

"I'm Deputy Sayce. So you didn't know that Mr. Kinsey's body was missing?" the deputy asked again.

"Nope. Not 'till you just told me."

"So could you tell me how your fingerprints might end up on items placed near the grave?" Barrett asked.

"Maybe. I was in the graveyard last night," Tommy said innocently.

"You were?" asked both cops simultaneously, it was almost comic.

"Sure. With Jade Cole and Chloe Kenworth."

"Really? Now that is interesting," said Barrett.

"Interesting how?" asked Tommy, puzzlement written all over his features.

"Interesting because of what we found at the grave … and what some poor bastard found earlier this morning. Very interesting," Barrett said.

"I'm not following ..."

"What were you doing in the graveyard, Tommy?" asked

Sayce.

"Havin' a party. We'd just buried our friend."

"A party by a grave? Not sure I like the sound of that, son," Barrett replied.

"It was something we promised each other. Stupid."

"Why would you do that? Why would two young guys even have that conversation?" asked Barrett.

"Because they both lost older brothers, Deputy. It affected them both very deeply," Tommy's mum replied.

"I'm sorry to hear that, ma'am," Barrett said. "Tommy, why would your prints be on a bottle of blood?"

"You found that?" Tommy laughed. "That was just a joke."

"Not a very funny one, son. I'm not laughing." Sayce looked cold at him.

"We were into horror movies, sir. It was a joke. We said we'd do it so we wouldn't get turned into zombies or something. It started out we'd sprinkle salt, but then it got more and more 'till it was blood. It wasn't serious, but we promised," Tommy explained.

"When did you leave?"

"About two in the morning, maybe a little earlier."

"Little late for a school night," Sayce said.

"I had special dispensation; I'd just been to my best friend's funeral."

"Did Chloe and Jade leave with you?" asked Barrett.

"No, Chloe left earlier, she didn't have dispensation and she freaked out anyway."

"You sure about that?"

"Yeah, she freaked and ran out, dude." Tommy chuckled.

"Why did she freak out, Tommy?" Barrett asked.

"I dunno, the graveyard at night? Go figure." Tommy shrugged.

"You didn't go after her? Make sure she was ok?"

"Hell no. Wandering off is her thing. Drama queen."

"She always freak out, too?"

"Sometimes, yes," Tommy replied.

"Really? What time did she freak out?"

"Midnight. A little after, maybe."

"Which way did she go?"

"Toward the town line. She lives out that way."

"Did you know that Chloe was found dead this morning?" asked Sayce casually, like he was asking the time.

Tommy went cold, mouth agape. His arms broke out in gooseflesh. Had he heard correctly? He sat down quickly before his legs gave out.

"What? What did you say?"

"I'm sorry, son. We didn't mean to shock you that way," Sayce said, more softly.

"H ... how?" Tommy asked.

"She was murdered, Tommy. I'm sorry," Barrett said.

"Fuck ... no." Tommy breathed.

"I'm sorry, Tommy. But I had to be sure you didn't know anything. Your reaction was important. You have to admit, it doesn't look good your prints being at the grave," Sayce explained.

"But surely ..." Tommy's mother began.

"When you said you were with Miss Kenworth last night ... well." Barrett went on.

"Surely you didn't think ..." gasped Tommy's mother.

"Not when I saw his reaction. No, ma'am. But knowing what we knew, it looked bad. Honestly, it still doesn't look too good as far as Jeffrey Kinsey is concerned, but we can't arrest you for having prints on a bottle."

"But I didn't do anything," insisted Tommy, tears running down his face.

"That's enough for now. Are you arresting my son?" asked his mother.

"Not right now, ma'am. Just don't leave town," Barrett replied.

"We weren't planning on it," Tommy's mother said, seeing the cops to the door.

****

Sayce and Barrett both visited Jade right after Tommy and had the events the boy had described verified. She sat at the kitchen table and sobbed when Deputy Barrett told her about Chloe's death. They offered their condolences and left her to her grief after only a few perfunctory questions. She couldn't handle any tougher questioning, that much was obvious. Through her grief she could barely utter a word, never mind assist in their enquiries. So they laid hands on her shoulder and left her to her misery.

She tried to call Tommy and was again told that he would return her call when he felt up to it. He was beginning to irritate her with his ignorance and worried her by his absence. It was beginning to feel like distancing and blame.

Now she sat at her desk in her room, absently stroking the marks on her arm where Tommy had worked the icons into her flesh. They were still warm.

Plans had begun to form in her mind; she might not need Tommy's aid but she would've liked to have him at her side when her plan came to fruition. Her plan had begun to form almost as soon as Deputy Barrett had talked about Chloe's death. She had needed to work hard to keep the smile from her lips at the memory of power surging through her.

She looked through her window at the darkening sky. Soon she would go out for a walk in the darkness; back to the graveyard perhaps, where she could order her thoughts better and weave her plans. Night had become her favourite time.

****

Father Cade walked up the rutted driveway toward the Kinsey farm with a hastened prayer running through his mind. He never usually made house calls unless someone was dying, but Marie Kinsey had not been to church in the last few weeks. Not since her son had died and it troubled the good Father to think of her grieving and bearing the pain of such a loss alone. He prayed to his god to lend him the words to give her solace in her time of confusion and bring her back to the flock. These were dangerous times with all the killings going on and the media all over town. Now was the time to draw strength from their numbers.

He said another quick prayer as he mounted the steps up to the porch. Tyrone Kinsey had given it a quick paint job before his son's memorial, but it still managed to look dilapidated somehow; like the entire structure would fall away from the house at a moment's notice. He knocked on the door and waited to hear Marie's footsteps on the other side. He had visited here many times in the past, not least of all during the arrangements of both her sons' funerals. He always found it to be a pleasant little home, like you might see on some home on the range movie. Not so now. Today it seemed a dark pall had descended on the place.

Marie answered the door after a few moments. Father Cade stood back from the door and exhaled sharply at the sight of the lady. Her once thick auburn hair was now greying at the sides and seemed to be thinning. She had lost a lot of weight since the funeral and she looked like she hadn't slept in a long while.

"Hello, Mrs. Kinsey," he said, stepping forward in lieu of an expected invitation to step inside but Marie didn't move aside. Neither did she answer him, just stared.

"Is everything okay, Marie?" he asked with some concern.

"I'm fine, thank you," she replied curtly, and after a pause.

"We haven't seen you in church lately. I was just coming to make sure you had everything you need, if there is anything we can do for you?"

"Nothing, thank you, Father. I've just been busy lately. I'm sure you can understand."

"Of course, of course. It has to have been hard on you," Cade said, his voice soft.

"It has, but I'm getting there."

"Is there any chance I could come in, perhaps we could chat a while?"

"I'm sorry, Father. The house is really upside down right now and I don't feel up to house guests," Marie said, perhaps a little too hurriedly.

"Ah. Of course. Then, might we see you in church on Sunday?" he asked, eyes darting to look over the lady's shoulder.

"Maybe … if I feel up to it … the people, I don't know if I can."

"In your own time, Marie. No rush. Might I come back for a visit next week perhaps?"

"We'll see. Look, I really have to get to some chores. Ty already thinks he's in with the pigs every time he walks in."

"Yes, I've taken up enough of your time … apologies …"

Marie closed the door before Father Cade could attempt a farewell. He stood for a few seconds, looking at his reflection in the glass in the door in some puzzlement. Marie Kinsey was never so offhand. It was almost disturbing. He turned finally and began his walk down the rutted driveway. He looked back over his shoulder at the house and scratched his head. His gaze went up from the closed door to the bedroom window, staring absently. As his gaze climbed the clapboard side of the house, he fancied he caught sight of a flitting movement from behind the net curtain. It was only a glimpse, perhaps a trick of the light as his focus sharpened. He was about to dismiss it when he thought he saw it again. Perhaps Marie was up there, watching to make certain he was leaving. He scratched his bald pate again, puzzling and hoping that the movement might happen again more distinctly. After several seconds it became apparent that it would not reappear, the phantom would not show itself. He turned and walked down the drive to the road, wondering what he may have seen in the Kinsey's house.

****

He wasn't disappointed when, at the end of the day, the girl had not been found. It had been a long while, and it would take a while longer. He knew they were in the general area but he couldn't just stumble upon her, not yet. Their little pencil circle had not opened wide enough on the map. Another three days, maybe four. He was determined to savour every second.

He was enjoying the country, beating his way through knots of wildflower and sedge and searching for something he knew could not be found. It didn't stop him from searching just as hard as the others though. Sweat dripped from his brow in the heat, as he looked over at his fellow searchers with a grim smile.

Coltraine had fit in well with his fellow volunteers as the day wore on, making easy conversation and joining in with their bad jokes. They had speculated wildly on the whereabouts of the girl and what might have become of her. He gave a detailed description of what he would do to the man who had harmed the girl which won him a few laughs and slaps on the back from his colleagues. Rumours concerning the state of young Chloe Kenworth's corpse coloured the talk. He joined in with that, too. If only the good old boys knew. At the day's end they trooped into Henrietta's, the only bar in town, drinking well into the evening. Townsfolk bought the boys drinks aplenty, drinks for the heroes. Inside Jack, Cal Denver was laughing.

****

"So, tell me exactly what you *are* doing, Sheriff. Because from here it seems not a hell of a lot!" Fielding criticised, as he did often. The sheriff sat at his desk and rubbed the bridge of his nose.

"I already told you, Frank. There's a way of doing these things ..."

"And those ways aren't getting results. Not in any way!"

"You think your boys are doing better, Frank? You'd be wrong," snapped Davies, his temper fraying.

"My boys are covering the miles; they're searching as well as they can. What do you want us to do, Sheriff ... bleed?" Fielding roared.

89

"Your guys are tramping through the search area. They could be destroying evidence. They shouldn't be out there!" Sheriff Davies shot back.

"They wouldn't be if your deputies could do their job right. It's been weeks since the first girl went missing, weeks! And you're still no closer to finding her *or* the man responsible."

"Neither are you. Who the fuck do you think you're talking to? What experience do you have in searches and manhunts, Fielding?"

"I know who I am, Davies. I'm the man who puts cash in your pocket to hold your annual Christmas parties. I'm the guy who paid for this office. I am the guy who paid for this fucking town. Don't you forget it, you ungrateful bastard," Fielding spat, incredulously.

"Yes, you're a society man, Fielding. In the big city you'd be a huge deal, right now you're just a pain in my ass. Now get out of my office!" Sheriff Davies shouted, jumping up from his chair and only just stopping short of throwing the man out bodily.

"Your office? Really? Remember that your position is a temporary one, Sheriff." Fielding warned.

"So is everyone's, Frank. Everyone dies sometime," Davies called as the door closed.

Fielding arrived home in a rage. He slammed his keys down on the table and stormed through to his study. *How dare Klimpt Davies speak to me in such a way?* He poured himself a healthy measure of liquor and drank it down in one before pouring a second. He had to think of a way to put the sheriff in his place.

Fielding had several contacts in the city, perhaps he could get the old bastard reprimanded or transferred. Maybe he could get him retired out completely. He had to do something. Then he hit on the perfect idea, a way to make sure the man suffered. He knew the sheriff had cut corners and not made the calls he should've done. Pride had stopped the man from following his own protocols. Now he would be punished. Fielding picked up the phone and dialled the number of a very old college buddy. A guy with power in the police service and jurisdiction that far outweighed Davies' own.

Within hours, the whole place would be swarming with men that were guaranteed to anger the sheriff beyond measure. As the connection was made and the phone started ringing, he smiled.

****

Jeffrey was forced to stay in his room all that day. Cops visited twice more and farm hands ducked in and out. It wouldn't do for Jeffrey to be seen. Even Father Cade had visited briefly that morning and been turned away. He heard his parents' pretence to normality through the floorboards and it sickened him. Lies upon more lies and all for his benefit. But what benefit?

The heat in his room was torture, adding to his already

considerable discomfort. Despite his mother's placatory words, his thoughts turned again and again to a solution to his predicament. He thought of all the books he'd read and the movies he'd seen, searching for a cure, but he found them all to be the fictions that they were. He'd read of fire, mutilation, and decapitations, all kinds of means to his end. He discarded each one; he just didn't have it in him to die twice.

He lay on his bed as the sun went down, watching a pair of flies squabbling around his lampshade. He saw his future in them. He fancied he could already feel his meat turning bad and he imagined the scurrying and squirming of creatures which, sooner or later, would burrow inside and lay their eggs. Such a horrible thought. He shuddered in disgust but still couldn't tear his eyes from the squabbling flies.

****

Through the raging conflict going on in his mind, Tyrone Kinsey had decided on avoidance. It was the only way to ease his troubled mind when he cast it in the direction of his son and so he didn't think about it. Questions still vexed him and he harboured suspicions that whatever was staying in his son's room was not his son. He was powerless to do anything about those suspicions. His wife's utter acceptance that her son was returned to her was enough to know this. He didn't have to ask Marie what her thoughts were to know what she believed. The way she had fallen into old routines, as though

Jeffrey were simply sick and recuperating. How could Tyrone be the one to shatter those illusions and break her heart all over again?

He stayed away from the house as much as he could. He wandered the fields until late into the evening, not returning until he was too exhausted to do anything else. He ate a swift dinner then went up to his room but the constant whirring of thoughts and fears circled his brain. Sleep didn't come easily these days. He would hear his son, or the thing that claimed to be his son, moving around in the bedroom across the landing. Marie would busy herself downstairs in the kitchen, readying utensils and food stuffs for the meals to come the following day. It was a mockery of normality and it was cloying. It felt almost like he had lost his wife–his sons, too. He might as well have lost his own life when his boys were taken but he lived, and he had problems. Usually he would sort through those problems, but how could this situation be sorted? This wasn't like any crisis he had ever known.

So he tried to rest while his over-active mind puzzled on the conundrum that had become his every day. Could he call the sheriff? No, Marie would never forgive him for what might come next. Could he seek solace in the counsel of Father Cade? Not likely. If the stories floating around the town and his work crew were to be believed, the preacher was even crazier than his wife. So … he was alone. Totally, completely. He seemed to be the one beacon of sanity in a world gone mad.

Poor Jeffrey

****

Del Foster pressed his foot hard into the floor and shifted up a gear, weaving through the traffic on the freeway. He was in a hurry, he always was. He was in a state of irritation, reading the papers and reading about murders which rightly he should have been informed of days before; deaths which closely resembled murders that he was investigating. He wasn't surprised that the local cops had chosen not to call the Feds in. He had been a cop himself and understood the feelings of resentment that his badge and suit could engender. He had felt those things himself at one time, but that time was over thirty years ago. He looked at himself in the rear view mirror, the heavy eyes and greying hair that looked like threadbare carpet. He was a wreck.

The resentment from the cops wouldn't be so irksome had it not been for the urgency of his situation. He had been working this investigation for over five years off and on, and yet he had got no closer to catching the killer responsible for these heinous crimes. Over thirty young men and women, all sharing the same type of injuries, and yet there was no evidence to say who was responsible for them. He had beaten his head against this brick wall for all this time; it had contributed to his smattering of sparse grey hair. He knew every face of every victim; he saw them each night before he slept. He imagined their rage, their grief, and in his turn he grieved. So the attitude of some uniform cop in some backwater town did nothing to appease his irritation.

94

He moved back down the gears as he slowed to a more sedate pace, the traffic thinned ahead. He turned his music down when his phone started dancing across the dashboard. Foster caught it just as it toppled off and scowled at the unknown caller icon on the display. "Be quick, I'm drivin' here," he growled into the receiver.

"Agent Foster, this is Tim Neeson. Our director has put me on your cannibal case," a voice said curtly on the end of the line.

"Oh, he has, huh?"

"Yes, he has. I am booked into the Cedars Motel on the edge of town. I'd really appreciate if you could come there and fill me in on the investigation so far."

"I'm sure you would," Foster growled.

"Good. I'll expect you here in a couple of hours," Neeson said, ignoring the sarcastic tone.

"You don't hang around, do you, Agent Neeson?"

"Never knowingly, Agent Foster," came the curt reply, then the line went dead.

Foster went on with his driving, jaw clenched tightly as his anger rose to still higher climes. He turned his music up and went back up through the gears. The beauty of being in the Feds ... there was no speed limit.

Almost exactly two hours later, Foster was pulling into the dusty car park of the Cedars Motel. It was a squat, two-floor clapboard house that couldn't accommodate more than a couple of visitors. He walked up to the porch and was about to press the buzzer when an officious looking man in a suit opened the door. "Agent Foster, I presume?" the man said curtly.

"Agent Neeson?"

"Christ no. He's inside. I'm Charles Spence. I'm the owner here."

"Ah. Is Neeson here?"

"Yes, he's been in his room since he arrived. He came in with a hell of a lot of computer stuff," Spence said.

"I'm not surprised. Can you tell him I arrived?" Foster asked.

"Of course, come in. Will you be staying, too?"

"Is there another motel in town?"

"Well, yes. There's a couple."

"Good. No offence, but I don't like the idea of sharing a house with colleagues." Foster smiled sardonically.

"Of course. Well, come in."

Foster followed the man into the boarding house and was instantly thankful he had told Spence he wasn't staying. The décor of the house was like someone's grandmother had chosen it, all flowers and frilly edges. To his left a doorway opened onto some kind of communal sitting room with a small TV in the corner. The chairs and sofa were as flowery as the walls, the effect was nauseous.

He heard Neeson before he saw him. His heavy footsteps sounded loud across the ceiling and down the stairs. When he appeared, Foster took an instant dislike to him. He wore light blue jeans with a hockey blazer. He was young with dark hair that looked like it needed a comb through it. A typical young man, Neeson walked over, hand outstretched and a bright smile on his lips.

"How are you, Agent Foster?" he said.

"I'm fine. Tired. You?"

"Yes, fine. Would you like a drink while we talk?"

"Damn fine idea, is there a bar close by?"

"Well, yes, but it's a bit public for the conversation we need to have."

"And here's a bit quiet. Let's go find that bar."

On the walk over to the bar, Neeson began a round of incessant questioning. Soon his voice was just an irritating buzz in his head as he took in his surroundings. The town seemed perfect for a kind of ending, like one of those quiet backwater towns where the world ends in the movies. It felt like he would reach some kind of conclusion here. Whatever shape that took.

He walked, looked up the street and smiled at its perfection. Then he turned his attention back to Neeson's litany of questions.

****

Over the next couple of weeks, Chloe watched everything change around town as the number of victims and missing girls grew. The sheriff and his deputies had given way somewhat to men in suits in the search for her killer and the grave robber. She had heard Sheriff Davies on a couple of occasions, arguing about some detail of the investigation.

These confrontations had often ended with the sheriff marching to the cordon line, his face beetroot red, the effect almost comical to her eyes. She laughed even harder when the sheriff cursed Frank Fielding for his interference, whatever that meant. She had seen Father Cade at the scene a few times early on, but it seemed the men in suits didn't appreciate his presence so he stayed away from the investigators now.

Specialists had scratched their heads over Chloe's remains, which had been shipped out to a facility out of town along with the remains of those victims whose families were lucky enough to know they would have them to bury, a place to lay a wreath.

She had heard the cops and Feds talking about a worrying lack of DNA evidence. They had established the cause of her death but failed to explain how a person might do what had been done to her without leaving a trace of themselves behind. They would find out soon. Of course Chloe knew, she could tell them exactly how the deed had been done, could take them right to the culprit. Except she was lying ragged and torn in a freezer somewhere.

She wandered through the town often, looking into the haunted and fearful eyes of those she'd known well, all of them shadowed by the events that had happened, were still happening in their midst. Two more bodies found, more missing since her and the mute girl had been killed and the townsfolk began to look to each other with suspicion. The more news that surfaced, the deeper the suspicion seeped into the town.

She watched Jade a little more, too. The girl worried her, the way she seemed so distracted all the time. At home she spent hours flipping through her tarot deck, absently searching the internet; looking only at sites dedicated to the dark side of the magicks. Jade would sit and mutter to herself, like inwardly she was having an argument. She didn't see Tommy anymore, she seldom saw anyone anymore.

Tommy. He had fallen furthest and it had broken Chloe's heart to see it. He had once been so carefree and fun loving. So up for anything, any mischief. He used to have a certain glint in his eye, especially when at the side of Jeffrey. They had burned so brightly. In the first days after her death she had watched him sitting at his desk, slicing away at the sigils on his arms with his silver knife. Plainly he wouldn't be satisfied until the images were totally obliterated.

The blood ran down his chest and arms but he kept on and on until each icon was utterly destroyed. Since then he had become hollow, empty, extinguished. He went to school, acted somewhat normally around normal people but Chloe could see the motions he was going through.

Watching in morbid curiosity again, she was spurred into action by her witnessing. As Tommy, Jade, and the entire town fell to pieces; as the cops and the investigators cast around hopelessly for a break in the case and the bodies piled up, Chloe was practicing. She was a ghost and sometimes, just sometimes, they learned to talk. Chloe had begun to learn in those days how to speak.

Poor Jeffrey

****

Jade stared out of her bedroom window, shuffling her tarot deck absently. It was a pursuit she had taken to since everything had happened. Chloe's death had shocked her beyond words. She now barely spoke to her mother, she rarely washed and her hair was an unkempt mess. She had not gone insane though, as her mother had feared. No, she was just deep in thought. She would wash, brush the kinks out of her hair and put on some fresh clothes, but not yet. It would interrupt her focus.

She held close those things that she saw as powerful, those things that might evoke the same feelings as the working had done over Jeffrey. The tarot had become her best friend showing her futures undreamed of and possibilities of resolution to her situation. In her mind the answer was simple, or getting to be simple.

She would have to attempt what Tommy had done to put things to rights, another working to put Jeffrey right and to bring back Chloe. It was the only way that she could fix herself. She had lost too many good friends in too short a time … she couldn't just let that go.

Now that she had a plan, she went and showered, put on fresh clothes and went to call Tommy. He had something that she would need.

****

"You know why I spend so much time in the bar, Neeson?" Foster growled as he sipped his drink.

"Couldn't tell you."

"Because this is where the stories are told, Tim. This is where people live their lives and tell their secrets."

"In the movies, maybe …" began Neeson.

"Screw the movies. If you just sit and listen, you'd be surprised what you can hear in a bar. A guy over there, see?" Foster nodded at a man with his back turned to them, his bald head red from the sun. "He's screwin' around with that guy's wife … and the guy knows it."

"So? How does that help us?"

"These are the people who know about the town, because *this IS* the town. You really don't get it, do you?"

"Frankly, no. If any of these men here were to give a statement it would be inadmissible, anything they said would be disbelieved. They're drunks!" Neeson scoffed.

"You think? This is where the nugget of the truth is found … then you look for the real evidence."

"That's worked well so far. Very well," Neeson said with sarcasm thick in his tone.

"Maybe not yet … not here. But I've been close to this guy a few times."

"Close, but not close enough."

"Closer than you'll ever get sitting at your computer with your cell stuck to your ear!" Foster countered.

"Perhaps, but if you didn't go around pissing off every deputy in town we might get a little closer."

"You think that's what I'm doing? Is this your first rodeo, Tim? You know as well as I do that they're never gonna help us, not if they can help it."

"Perhaps they would if you could be a little more diplomatic?"

"And maybe we could get further if you got your hands dirty once in a while," Foster snapped back.

And round and round the argument circled, all the time Neeson failed to notice what Foster was hearing. In the general hubbub of the bar he was hearing snippets of conversation, covering his eavesdropping with the argument. None in the bar would suspect that he was listening in, as seemingly engaged in the argument as he was.

There were secrets in this town; there were in every town, and here is where some of those secrets might be revealed.

****

"We have invited the stench of the cities into our community and their sin follows. See how unlawful they are, how uncouth. They sully our streets with their very presence. Do you not see? I have been in their cities; I have walked through their streets. I have seen the seas of iniquity that these people bathe in. I have seen decent communities like this very one, decimated into hell holes of crime, deprivation, and sinful conduct. I would not have that here." He railed, sweat pouring from his brow and dripping from the end of his nose. The tirade had left him red faced and panting.

Throughout this portion of his sermon he had glared at the sheriff and the mayor, his resentment of their acceptance of the city-folk plain to see.

Father Cade's sermons had been getting ever wilder as time had gone on. Secretly, he had not slept well since the disappearances of the girls had begun. Lately he didn't sleep at all. He walked around the town until late into the night, Exodus at his side. He searched every nook and cranny, feeling like it was his responsibility to at least attempt to keep the townspeople safe. To no avail, more had disappeared and more had been murdered. Worse still, tourists were arriving in town by the coachload and bringing with them thieves and drunks. The priest looked around the town and remembered the quiet suburb he had been assigned to right at the beginning of his career in the collar.

He had been just a young man then and had recently made the step up to take his own flock. He had instantly fallen in love with the area and its inhabitants. The people were friendly and their children respectful; it was a god-fearing congregation who enjoyed his fresh-faced approach to his sermonising. He was engaging, friendly. Just what the neighbourhood needed.

It took a few years for the cracks to appear in the façade. Families moved out and new ones moved in, these ones less apt to attend their church. It wasn't long before the old attendees stopped going to church and never walked the street by night. On the main street appeared graffiti and burned out cars. Crime began to reign in the parish and

Father Cade felt powerless to do anything about it. There was a spate of shootings in the area connected to a drug and prostitution ring that had sprung up in the community. After a drive-by shooting just outside the church he gave statements to the press and appealed for the citizens of his parish to be calm, to stop the killing, but his calls fell on deaf ears. There was more killing, more death as if in spite of the priest's words. It left him bereft and frustrated. Soon after that he was moved away from that community and sent to work by the sea, where he might enjoy the sun and relax a little. He never truly relaxed though. He was always on the lookout for the devil creeping close to him.

Here he was now, his presence looming large over the town. This time, though, Father Cade would not allow it to stand. He had been blind before, in that community he had loved so much. Not so now. If he had to wander the streets all night and never sleep again it is what he would do to keep his streets unsullied. That was his vow.

He looked out over the congregation. Sheriff Davies was as red faced as the priest, his ire at the man's attacks as plain as the priest's resentment of him and his actions. Some members of the congregation looked on in rapt attention, still more simply looked uncomfortable. Father Cade nodded to himself and ended the service in his now traditional way. "My Lord is my shepherd, I shall not want, he maketh me down to lie in green pastures …"

****

He had taken more girls from town, and from towns all over the district. Anywhere within the distance of a short drive. He had scattered their remains far and wide, surely not all of them would be discovered. He had never eaten so well. In the past he had always felt threatened, sooner or later. Here he felt at home. The cops were no closer to him now than they had been right at the very beginning when he had predicted his stay would last hours, not weeks. He had been good. Very good. He had stuck to his usual methods, remained calm and detached. No one would ever suspect the fiction that was Jack Coltraine. He was too dumb, too innocent and sweet natured. Through those early days of searching, he had been easily folded into the new dynamic of town life. Now those who searched were heroes; those who had uncovered remains were legendary. Coltraine had become a legend just four days in.

His group was searching in the north, right around the state line and close to the highway. They hadn't expected to find anything that day, they hadn't in the previous days, but a journalist and photographer had tagged along that day and lent a fresh gusto to their work. For hours they searched through the undergrowth when suddenly the journalist got her story and Coltraine got his face, grief stricken and pale, splashed across the cover of three different newspapers. In town, that made him famous. Of course there had been photographs since yet none had captured the raw emotion like the despair in Coltraine's eyes upon the discovery of little Clare Harvey, poor mute Clare Harvey.

Cal Denver was well satisfied. It wasn't a performance because Coltraine honestly was grief stricken. There was just nothing that he could do to stop him. He was weak and the medicines had failed him. Cal was in control.

****

Foster walked around the scene for what felt like the hundredth time, and he would wander around it a hundred more if need be. This was his process; it was how he made some kind of sense of the insensible. Though the body had been removed some hours ago he could still see the way she had been arranged, the position of the body; not just dumped and left for scavengers but laid down carefully. This was not the work of some deranged lunatic; there was something behind this, some kind of ritual or belief structure. It was the same at all the scenes from this murderer, aside from the times when he had been disturbed. It was all too familiar. His heart sank.

Of course he had traced murderers many times before. He'd seen his share of difficult and drawn out investigations, but nothing even remotely like this one. It had taken him across four state lines and led him to the remains of so many bodies yet he was no closer to the culprit. How was it possible? He wandered around the cordoned off area, looking at the ground and up into the trees as if the man he was searching for might lie there. Of course, that would be far too much to ask for.

Neeson watched Foster impatiently. He wanted to get back to the motel where he could get some internet coverage. He hated working in the sticks, disconnected from what he considered civilisation. He didn't like being unable to use technology, it stymied his effectiveness and Foster's prevarication was irksome.

Over the first few days of the investigation they had each built up a healthy dislike of each other's methods, and each other as men if truth were told. They were total opposites in nature. Neeson wanted to check and recheck facts, Foster needed to be out on the ground doing the legwork. Totally incompatible!

Neeson began to wonder if he could do better alone. Of course in the short time they had been in town he had ruffled feathers, he had put noses out of joint, but not in the way Foster was. It seemed the old man was willfully alienating himself from the town cops. Surely only a matter of time before he was on the wrong side of the ordinary townsfolk too. He had to be curbed.

As he waited, he walked around the car, trying to find some signal in this hell hole. He found a small area where he could make a call and dialled. After three rings, his director picked up.

****

The disappearances were now murders and the town was besieged by city-folk come to take a look around the place, media types and morbid tourists. For Tyrone Kinsey the news was far more disturbing. Worse still were the stories that came from the searches and the men who had found the remains of the girls. Cannibalised was a word often used, probably overheard from one of the white suited, alien kinda looking folks that had arrived with the first finding. That word brought strange associations for Ty; cannibalised meant a crazy animal, fit only for the butcher. One that will eat its own. He shook his head to rid himself of the dark images that the word brought to mind.

He wandered the fields, as was his custom now. His thoughts still turned over his wife and his son, or the thing that was now his son. As if it wasn't bad enough that Jeffrey had risen from his grave and probably right now was sitting in his bedroom, larger than life, now girls were disappearing and showing up dead and half eaten. Surely that could be no coincidence? But what could he do about it?

He had already dismissed the idea of going to the sheriff; the man would think him crazy to suggest his dead son was the one responsible for such heinous crimes. He had dismissed Father Cade too, the man was in the middle of some breakdown of his own, the way he wandered the town at all hours and muttered to himself. Ty would've rejected the rumours as just that, but he had seen the old priest for himself and seen the degradation of the man. It was sad to see the man so in disarray with his hair gone wild and that strange muttering, like he was trying to talk himself into or out of something.

So that left him alone to sort through his problem. What to do about Jeffrey. He had toyed with the idea of killing him; of taking him out into the back yard like a sick dog and shooting him. He couldn't bring himself to even pick up his rifle. How would one go about killing his own son when that son was meant to be dead already?

He wandered the fields, totally alone and making a pretence of normality. He accepted it as his new lot in life. Sudden tears sprang forth, they often did these days. He needed a way out ... quickly.

****

Frank walked around the town with a smile on his face. He was the only man who did smile these days. A pall had fallen over the place since the first bodies had been found and normality carried on in a hushed, almost funereal way. Where there would ordinarily be a hubbub of chatter, there was a quiet he hadn't felt before. But none of this could touch Fielding at that moment. He had made plans, he had set himself goals and each one had far exceeded his expectations. He had intended to be some kind of irritation to the sheriff since their argument, never could he have expected to be such a thorn in the man's side. He had intended to make the sheriff and his men appear totally inept, impotent compared to the things that he alone could achieve. It was the sheriff's own fault. Fielding could very easily have had the man's job, but that would be too easy. No, what Fielding had done was far worse.

The Feds had arrived in town with their vans and equipment, making calls on cellular phones and collating information about these killings and other similar ones. Apparently there was quite a dossier of deaths and the sheriff's lack of co-operation could potentially have cost the men in suits time and maybe even an arrest. Fielding was in the office the day the Feds' leader had threatened the sheriff with his own imprisonment if his delay cost any more lives. It had filled Frank with a feeling of total satisfaction to see the fat old bastard squirm in his seat.

Then the coup de grace ... the day that Jack Coltraine, one of Fielding's own men came out of the woods with his tale to tell. It hadn't been the sheriff's men *or* the Feds that had found the remains of the little girl. It had been Frank's boys. Oh, how that must've pricked at the good sheriff's pride. When Fielding had received the call to let him know what had happened, he broke out a decanter of his very best wine to celebrate. He had gotten a little drunk on the wine *and* the pride he'd gained from making Klimpt Davies look utterly foolish. It affirmed his place in town society as the man of deeds, not words.

Now he had to decide on his next course of action. His boys remained in the field, searching for more bodies or perhaps even a survivor. What could he do next to infuriate the sheriff even more ... and perhaps encourage the relic to disappear completely? Perhaps if he found the killer? He sighed and wondered if that might just be possible, too.

****

Jade banged on Tommy's door impatiently. She knew his parents would be out and that he'd be alone in the house. She was done with his ignorance. He hadn't returned her calls, emails, or hastily written notes that she'd posted in his locker. If they crossed paths in the school hall or the street he would stare right through her like she was made of glass. She was done with it.

She kicked the door and slammed her fist against it one more time then resorted to plan B. She had seen his pale face at the window when she approached the door, if he wanted her to make a scene in front of the whole neighbourhood then so be it. She stepped back away from the door and looked up, shielding her eyes from the sun with her hand.

"Tommy! Tommy! I know you're in there, lemme in," she cried, then waited a second or two. There was no movement at window or door, so she went on. "Tommy! You bastard, you just gonna leave me screamin' out here? You want the neighbours hearin' this?" Again, nothing. "Are you really gonna leave a pregnant girl out here in the street?! she screamed.

That did the trick. The door was flung open and Tommy, sweating and ashen faced, bundled her into the house and slammed the door behind him.

"What the fuck are you thinking?" he screamed.

"I got your attention, didn't I?" She grinned. "You look awful."

"What I look like ain't none of your business," Tommy snapped.

"I've been worried, Tom. With Chloe gone I ... you know?"

"Yeah? How do you think I feel?"

"I tried calling you. I wanted to help but ..." Jade left the statement hanging, so it was only in part a lie.

"You can't help. Nobody can."

"Stop being pathetic. I've got an idea." Jade smiled.

"Yeah? Well, I'm not interested."

"You don't even know what it is yet." She frowned.

"I'm done with our ideas. They were stupid. They were dangerous," Tommy said flatly.

"Dangerous? How?"

"You've seen Jeff?"

"No ... have you?"

"Nope. But you saw what our great plan did to him, right?"

"We got it wrong. We can put that right, though ... I ..."

"You can't. No one can," Tommy cut in.

"I can. I promise. I've done some checking."

"Jade, haven't we done enough?" Tommy sighed.

"We haven't, no. All I need is to double check some details," Jade insisted.

"It's too late. There's nothing ..."

"I can put Jeff right, I know I can. I can bring Chloe back, too. I just need your book, that's all."

"No way. It's bad news," Tommy said.

"I can do it. I know I can. I can make it all better."

"You can't, Jade. We were wrong!"

"I don't need you. Just your book," Jade said, a sudden ice in her tone.

"You can't have it," Tommy insisted.

"If you won't give it I can just take it," purred Jade, almost seductively.

"You won't find it."

"I don't need to find it. It's already calling out to me." Jade smiled and headed for the stairs.

"Have you gone crazy?" Tommy cried, incredulous.

"Nope. And I'll prove it," Jade replied casually as she climbed the stairs. Her prize was indeed calling her, after a fashion. With Tommy's protests ringing in her ears, she went unerringly to his room and over to the bed; she pulled the box from underneath. He protested more, she ignored him and placed the box on his desk.

She opened the lid and regarded the book which lay within like a long hidden sacred text. When she laid her fingertips on the grimoire, it tingled under her touch. She saw now in her mind the uses the book had been put to, the uses it could yet be put to. Magic, however botched the working had been, had opened up a portion of her that she never knew existed. Now she had the proof of that place as the book fed her more images, more emotion. She took the book from the box and stepped to the door; Tommy barred the way.

"I won't let you take it," he warned.

"You don't want it and you won't stop me," she spat back.

"Oh, won't I?" he hissed.

"I don't think so." She smiled and stepped past him. "I have become greater than you now," she whispered as she went. Tommy, as she had predicted, did nothing to stop her.

****

His lips moved slightly as he walked with his little dog at his side. If anyone but his most devoted acolytes cared to walk close to him, they would hear the prayers he uttered as an almost constant litany. Thankfully there was no one to hear him; no one to wonder at the good Father's sanity.

He walked in the fields around the town. He told himself that he was aiding in the search for the girls, or better still the killer of the girls. In truth he knew that he was searching for remains. He was also looking for the source of the evil which had oozed into the fabric of his quiet life. He hated the darkness that recent events had brought to the town, he wanted it gone.

He walked down the lane and came abreast of the Kinsey farm gate. He thought back to the last time he had visited Marie Kinsey. The sight of the lady had haunted him but the tragic happenings around the town had taken all of his attention. The strange flitting movements in the upstairs window had also played on his mind, yet he had done nothing to investigate. He hadn't even told the sheriff about what he may have seen in that upper window.

He turned into the gateway and began the walk up the rutted driveway. Looking up the slight incline, he saw Ty Kinsey's truck parked in the space between the house and the outhouse where he kept his tools. The priest never quite knew what to make of Mr. Kinsey. He was neither religious nor a non-believer, he was nice enough but the priest often wondered if he perhaps drank a little much or beat his wife where the bruises wouldn't show. Since their first son's death, Marie Kinsey had become withdrawn; since Jeffrey's death she was a recluse. Father Cade sometimes believed that he was the only one who might notice these things. In the current circumstances those thoughts were amplified. In a time of ungodliness, he must stand as a beacon in the darkness.

He approached the house, watching the upstairs windows for any sign of the flickering movement the like of what he had seen those few weeks ago. Too soon he was under the awning of the porch and could no longer see the blind windows, having seen nothing other than empty glass reflecting the blue skies. He knocked on the door and waited for it to be opened. After a long while he heard Marie Kinsey unlocking the door. When it was opened his senses were assailed with the overpowering smell of lemon air freshening sprays. He took a step back, momentarily unable to breath. Marie looked less gaunt than she had, in fact she looked almost happy as she stood in the doorway.

"Hello, Father. What can I do for you?" she asked.

"I ... er ... I came to check ... to check you were alright," Cade stuttered, trying to gather his thoughts.

"We're fine ... or as fine as we can be. Thank you for your concern."

"We still haven't seen you at church," Cade said, the implication left in the air between them.

"I haven't been to church since ..." Marie said flatly.

"Are you sure everything is okay?" Cade asked, his brow furrowed. This was not like the Marie Kinsey he knew.

"Like I said, as fine as it can be, Father."

"May I come in for a moment?" Cade asked, not really wanting to enter the house. Underneath the stench of the fresheners was something else, something he couldn't work out.

"I'm afraid not. My husband is doing some building work inside," Marie explained.

"Ah ... is Ty coping alright, then?"

"Better than me ... he's a good man, strong man," Marie replied, her own brow furrowing now.

"Of course. Well, I'll leave you be, then. If you need anything ..." the priest stuttered, feelingly suddenly awkward in the woman's presence and with the smell he couldn't quite place around her.

Marie closed the door and Father Cade turned to walk down the steps. Again he turned to look up to the windows as he left the Kinsey land down the drive. As he looked around, again he thought he saw some flitting movements behind the curtains like someone had stepped aside quickly, afraid of being seen. He stopped and looked at the window in the hope that the figure may reappear, but it didn't. Disappointed and just a little bit relieved, he turned and walked back the way he had come. He was vexed by the strange phenomena behind those windows, further still by Marie Kinsey's behaviour. Yet, now that he was in the fresher air it was the smell that wafted from the house that troubled him more.

****

Agent Neeson had never had a case such as this one. Not many had. He was young and hungry, one of the best talents that the next generation of agency operatives could boast. Foster was older and way more experienced. It was hoped that the blend of experience and hunger might aid the case and bring it closer to some kind of resolution. It hadn't helped much.

If only his director could see what the situation on the ground was. That the man who was supposed to be there to support him was actually throwing up road blocks at every turn. Foster resisted almost everything that Neeson suggested and he grew weary of it. Yet the director still had faith in the legend that was Del Foster. It was ridiculous.

Of course, Neeson was ambitious. He had trained to be in the Feds since he was a youngster and achieved his dream by being taken into MIT. He had worked his way through their intense training and was in the top few scholars of his time. There was no information he hadn't absorbed and yet he was here, impotent. It sickened him. If he had his way he would have drafted in behavioural analysts and psychologists, PR and media agents to handle that end of things, but Foster would have none of it. The analysts would only confuse matters with their psychobabble, attention which would normally be rapt on the evidence would be drawn away because some suspect didn't fit their imaginary profile. Similarly he knocked back the media and PR people, the last thing Foster needed was a bunch of newspaper hacks spooking the killer into running. And so Neeson was stymied. He had even attempted to draw up some kind of profile of his own but Foster had thrown it in the trash. Stubborn old fool!

Now he sat and tapped away at his keyboard, reviewing what evidence he had collected from the databases he could access. He had reports and evidence files from over three hundred different cases to sort through and place in categories, it was tedious. If any other cases, earlier investigations, had missed a connection and there was some sort of devastating piece of evidence the search would be worthwhile. Already he had a few good possibilities on the screen. But it was still the current situation that vexed him.

There was no evidence, nothing to use as a nail to hang suspicion on. The only hard evidence was found at Jeffrey Kinsey's grave, but it wasn't enough to tie young Jade and Tommy to the murders. They were a different order of evil, those murders; doubly so because they were so clinical. If you didn't think too hard about the method of killing.

Clinical simply because of the lack of DNA evidence. What Doctor Prentzler had failed to explain had taken the finest pathologists with the latest technologies in the most modern facilities mere days to explain. Yes, the girls had been eaten by another human being, that much was certain. That in itself was a wonder, that a person could subdue and consume a live person with nothing but his teeth. Not impossible, but highly improbable.

The real mystery lay in the lack of DNA; no saliva, no sliver of tooth or stray foreign hair. Heads were scratched all around until one test, one tox analysis showed a minute trace of acid in one of the girls. Once found in one body, the same element was quickly found in the rest. That was when they finally understood how it might be possible to make himself invisible.

Now, though, they were at an impasse. Girls had disappeared and bodies were recovered; the searches continued and the agents butted heads with the sheriff and his men. It made for an uncomfortable investigation, and Neeson had the impression that he wasn't being told everything.

****

Blessed ignorance. It seemed to have come easily to Jeffrey's parents. There was so much that they turned a blind eye to, things that Jeffrey couldn't ignore. He couldn't because it had become his life.

When he was younger he was accused of stealing penny sweets with Tommy from the local grocery store. It had begun with a simple dare but had soon grown into a sort of morning ritual. They had been discovered by the owner and their parents called. Of course, Jeffrey's parents could scarce believe that their son, their good boy, would do such a thing. As his parents argued with Sheriff Davies and the kindly store owner, he and Tommy snickered behind their backs.

Two weeks of baking heat in his sweatbox bedroom had been unkind. His premonition with the flies had soon come to pass and now he felt a constant scurrying and squirming under his flesh. Sometimes he saw movement, life now using his dead cage as a home. It didn't hurt, didn't even itch; it just was as it was. More distressing was watching his skin darken as its substance broke down, forming open sores which oozed putrefaction. He could no longer sit or lie down, every time he did represented another dark patch of skin; more dead flesh.

Worse, he could feel his brain dying, liquefying in its pan and running out of his nose like snot. With each passing day he lost a little more coherence in his thoughts and movements, his speech was becoming more slurred as his tongue rotted and the message from brain to lips became lost in confusion. Recently he had caught sight of himself in a mirror and was sickened by the wretched sight staring back at him.

All of this his parents were able to ignore.

The stench could not be overlooked. Though he showered with strong smelling soap and drowned himself in aftershaves and deoderisers, though he burned sweet smelling candles and his mother sprayed air freshener constantly, the stench of rot and putrescence could not be concealed.

It clung to Jeffrey, emanated from his every pore, his every breath. He was miserable, lurching around his room like a badly oiled automaton with no other purpose than his body's refusal to lie down and die.

Soon he hoped to be found out. He had seen Father Cade looking up to the windows and thought he had been seen. Soon, he hoped his parents would come to their senses and dash his brains out. Soon, he hoped to be released from this blessed ignorance.

****

Chloe was following Jade a lot now. She watched Coltraine spying on Jade each night as she walked between the gravestones. She didn't know his name or his history but soon she would know enough; perhaps too much. He wasn't there every night, but most evenings he was there; wrapped in the shadows. Jade was too much a creature of routine and it would soon get her killed. Chloe looked into his eyes, he had changed since he had taken her. There had been gentility about him when he had comforted her, even as he had bitten into her. There was no sense of that about him now. He watched Jade with an animalistic hunger, a desire that drifted

121

from him like an odour. It sickened her. Jade was too distracted by her thoughts to notice the eyes upon her. Chloe had seen the grimoire on the desk in Jade's room and here it was now in her hands. The very sight of the ancient book filled Chloe with an irrational fear; she felt the evil coming off the artefact in waves. It filled her with dread to see it in Jade's room and to watch her so entranced by it. Soon, she might have the strength to show Jade her presence and warn her of the danger she faced by simply turning those pages. Not possible yet, she didn't know how.

Chloe breathed a sigh of relief when Jade made for home. She watched the would-be killer turn away in the opposite direction. Safe for one more night. Lucky. She followed Jade to her door, just to be certain of her safety, then she made a snap decision. One way that might just save Jade's life.

****

Jeffrey stood at the window, desperately trying to order his incoherent thoughts. He watched his father in the driveway, packing tools into the outhouse before he came in for lunch. Jeffrey had to speak to him shortly, he had to get him alone.

That day, Jeffrey had been filled with a certainty that he hadn't felt since his resurrection. He felt an endgame was coming and he knew in his marrow that it would involve him in some way. He didn't know where these feelings came from, just that they were there and that he had to somehow get his parents away from the house, if only for the night.

That was the part of his thinking that was difficult, how to persuade his father. His mushed brain could not conceive of an argument or work quickly enough to debate with his father. The only option open to him seemed to be honesty, to tell his father the whole sorry tale from beginning to end, or as far to the end as he could. Even Jeffrey couldn't tell how this was going to end.

He watched his father finish up with his work and stretch his back. He could see the sheen of sweat shining on his father's forehead and wished he could go outside and help finish up his chores like he did when he was alive. He was still trying to figure a pretext to get his father to talk to him.

An hour later and the issue was fixed as Tyrone Kinsey knocked on his door and entered with a plate of roast beef and potatoes. It was the first time in a few days that Tyrone had been in the boy's room and he found him much changed. His features seemed to be running down his face like liquid, his hair falling out in uneven clumps. The smell that rose from him was almost unbearable, how Marie could stomach holding him close was a mystery to him. The old man smiled at his son as he entered, although it pained him to do so. A smile was an expression that was unfamiliar to Ty lately; it had been a long time since he'd had cause to smile.

"I need to speak to you, Dad," Jeffrey said, his voice hoarse.

"You need to eat your food first," Tyrone replied, trying to act in some semblance of normality.

"I'm ... not that hungry," Jeffrey replied, smiling at his

father humourlessly.

"Still, your mother made it special-like."

"I know … doesn't do me any good though. I can't even taste it anymore." Jeffrey moaned.

"You don't eat much, huh?"

"Not at all … I'm not even hungry … ever."

Tyrone moved over and sat on the bed next to where his son stood. He was never one for shows of love or emotion but he rested a hand on his son's shoulder in an attempt at comfort. Or perhaps to show the boy/creature that its pretence was still believed. "Never hungry?"

"Never."

"Look, Jeff … I gotta ask this, just … you know …?"

"What is it, Dad?"

"Well, these murders lately. They're … they're nothing to do with you, right?" Tyrone felt lame for asking as if he expected an admission.

"Dad! Fuck no … what do you think of me?" Jeffrey exclaimed.

"Well … I've been giving that question a lot of thought since you came back here. I wondered what the hell you were, whether you were even my boy. I wondered whether I shouldn't just kill you all over again or somethin'. Fact is, I don't know what to make of all this," Tyrone said quietly.

"So why didn't you just kill me?" asked Jeffrey.

"How could I?" Tyrone laughed mirthlessly. "Your mother was a wreck when you went away, and then you came back and she was so happy, so relieved. How could I take that away? Even if I thought you were a demon or some other such evil thing, how could I hurt your mother all over again?"

"And you thought I was this killer, and still didn't wanna do anything?"

"I didn't know what to think … but I think you were fixin' to tell me somethin', weren't you?"

"I was. I was gonna ask you to do something for me," Jeffrey said, looking at the floor. "Now I don't think you will."

"What is it? What do you need?"

"Dad … I have to leave again …"

"Leave? Where you gonna go?"

"I gotta die again, Dad. This is unnatural, it was an accident. I can't stay around like this, but I know Mama ain't gonna let me just … go … so I need to be alone."

"But … why?"

"Look at me, Dad. Look, smell … it isn't right, is it?"

"Well … no, I guess not … but …"

"Please, Dad. You already said you can't do it. Well, sometime soon I think something's gonna happen and I'm part of it."

"What do you mean, son?"

"I don't know. Just … I have a feeling."

"So, what do you need me to do?"

"Take Mama away for a few days, go on vacation … whatever. Just don't be here. I think, if you're here it'll be dangerous for you both."

"Now just hang on a minute …"

"Dad, I mean it," Jeffrey said, his tone serious.

"How do you know anything's gonna happen?"

"Because … I think when you're dead, I think you can see things … future things … I think I still can … kinda."

"You mean you can see the future?"

"No … only possibilities. And I can feel the town, it's not good."

"Well, I gotta admit …" Tyrone began.

"Please, Dad. Just take Mama away."

Tyrone hesitated but held Jeffrey's stare. After a second's thought he nodded once, then stood.

"I guess I can do that for you, son."

"Could you do something else for me?" Jeffrey asked.

"Course I can, son."

"Please … don't remember me like this. This was never how I wanted to be. And don't come say goodbye, just go and let me do whatever it turns out I have to do."

"Okay, son." Tyrone sighed, sudden tears pricking his eyes. He left the room without looking back, vowing to keep his promise to his son.

****

The town hall was at the east end of town, its white marble built in affectation of the great buildings in Europe with deep steps and a colonnade. It had been built a century and a half previously and paid for by the Fielding family, of course. That morning the sun shone and the skies were a perfect blue. Frank Fielding stood on those steps and beamed into a camera, flanked by Agent Del Foster and Sheriff Davies. It was a picture that he would rerun on his video player at home many times, admiring the cut of his suit and his easy manner with the press folks gathered on the street before him. He knew that the scene would be broadcast that night and it would be his smile that would appear on millions of TV sets countrywide. He would be the face of the investigation, his name would be the remembered one.

He had dressed in his white suit and had his hair cut and had shaved twice, just to be sure he would look good for the camera. Now, standing on the steps that his forebears had built, he felt like the mayor himself.

"Are you closing in on a suspect? Is there any advance being made in the investigation?" called out one of the reporters in the front row. Fielding looked down and flashed her a smile. He admired her smart pinstripes momentarily.

"I'm sure Agent Foster will be able to tell you about any gains being made. For the town, all we can say is that our folk here will assist in any way we can and I'm certain Sheriff Davies feels the same way I do," Fielding said in his booming, public voice. The sheriff made to speak, but the agent had already begun his run down of recent developments. Frank smiled wider, it was perfect. It wasn't like Fielding liked the agent overmuch; he didn't like the Feds being in town, but it was a necessary evil. Anything that would humiliate the sheriff was a good thing.

"How are these murders affecting the town?" asked a different questioner this time.

"We are bearing up well," Fielding said, again cutting off the sheriff. "We come together in times of hardship. We support the families who have lost their sisters and their daughters. This is what we do round here."

And on, and on. Fielding would laugh later, as he watched Davies attempt to speak time and time again, only to be cut off by either Frank or the agent. He looked ridiculous, standing there with his surly expression growing ever redder. Fielding would never forget the way the sheriff had looked at him when he walked away, the murderous rage in his eyes might have floored a less confident man.

He was satisfied with his manipulations; they had got him to where he wanted to be. Soon, hopefully after this whole mess was cleared up and forgotten, there would be an election and he would be voted mayor because of his acts during these days. He had to be seen as the strong will that would bring down whatever evil was in the town. He had to be seen as the one doing something. In short, he had to find the killer himself.

****

Father Cade walked home with Exodus, the sight of Marie Kinsey burned into his mind and the smell of whatever it was underneath the air fresheners seared into his nostrils. His instincts recognised the undertones, had smelled the stink

128

before, but the naming of it evaded him. Perhaps the associations were not good; he had seen many horrors in his life before he had taken the cloth. He was once a soldier, a leader of men and a taker of arms. The things his senses had been assaulted with then were beyond his will to describe even to himself.

The flitting movements behind the curtains were more troubling still. What was it in the room beyond? His interest had been mildly piqued when he had first seen it, now his suspicion seemed to be confirmed and it vexed him. What was he to do?

He looked down and asked the question of his dog but the mutt just looked at him, head cocked and tongue hanging out as he panted. No answers to be found there. The priest sat in his chair and sipped at a glass of liquor, something to calm his nerves. He wondered if what he was seeing was innocent, just a trick of the light as a cloud passed over the sun. Maybe Ty Kinsey was up there, doing his building work. There could be any number of innocent explanations for what he may or may not have seen.

Like an irritation that wouldn't go away though, at the back of his mind was the nagging fear of the town succumbing to sin. It had happened before in one of his parishes, why not this one?

He decided he had to put his mind at ease and dialled the number. The voice at the other end of the line sounded irritated to hear the priest's voice. He had done nothing to endear himself to the sheriff of late yet he still hoped that the sheriff would hold just enough respect for him to go and look around the Kinsey house. If there was nothing to see, fair enough. If there was something there, however, he may yet save the town's soul.

****

Sheriff Davies was an old warhorse; he'd been around the block more than once or twice. No matter what Agent Del Foster believed of him, or that rat Frank Fielding, he was a good cop. In his younger days he'd worked the big city beats, he had seen his fair share of pointless death and madmen. Okay, he was never agency material, he would admit that readily, but he had certainly not been in the backwaters all his life. He was a veteran of the old guard; he knew enough to realise that sometimes in these types of cases it could be one quirk of luck that might blow an investigation open wide. Sometimes it was a nugget of evidence overlooked or a face out of place. More often it was no more than a piece of skewed fortune. Sheriff Davies knew this because he was an old-timer.

So he wasn't taking too kindly to the way the Feds, Neeson and Foster, had come along and taken over his investigation. They walked all over his jurisdiction like it meant nothing to him. He had taken a particular dislike to the young one, Neeson; officious, odious little bastard he was. At least Davies could relate to the older man. They were alike, stood on the same ground. Their rivalry was one of professional pride and expected in a way. It had been the same when he was in the big city, the Feds showed up and the ranks would close. But the kid, he was one slimy little toad. Davies could imagine him with tongue firmly attached to his superior's butthole. He had seen guys like that in the force; okay in the office when confronted with reams of reports and details, but put them in the field with a criminal and it was a far different story. Now Foster, he was a man that the old sheriff could understand. Yes, they would butt heads, but at least they would get the damn job done!

Klimpt Davies had been a good cop for forty years; he'd done his turn on the beat and been a detective in the big city. He'd been respected by his colleagues on the force and even some of the criminals seemed to have some kind of perverse professional admiration for him. He was fair, he knew when to go in softly and when to go in smashing heads.

Some of his old colleagues saw his transfer to the sticks as a kind of retirement, an acknowledgement that he was getting too old to do proper police work, but that was far from the truth. In his years he had seen many things but nothing like the escalation of violence he had seen in his last five years in the big city. He could no longer count on the fingers of one hand the number of fellow cops that had died in the line of duty. In those last five years there had been countless. He had prided himself on rarely having to draw his weapon. In those last five years he had fired his gun on five occasions and killed only twice. The last one had broken his heart.

On an evening investigation, reports had come in of

trespassers in the warehouse district and he had come under fire as he looked around the area. He ran and found cover behind a collection of bins, bullets grazing the walls overhead and around him. He took out his weapon and returned fire, unable to see a way out without firing off a few shots. He knew back up would be on the way after the first shots, but he daren't take any chances. He reloaded and began shooting again as more shots traced across the wall and pinged off the bins in front of him. Then, all went quiet as he heard a thumping sound akin to a sack full of grain toppling over. He poked his head over the bins cautiously and saw his attacker lying on the floor, blood pooling underneath. He approached the form, kicking the pistol which lay next to the right hand out of its reach. He crouched and turned the hooded figure and his world broke in two. Lying on the floor in such a damp alley, his blood leaking out into the gutter, was a boy no older than fourteen. It was enough to near break a man's mind. He carried on for a few more months but he knew that he was a liability. He could still do a job but now the darkness of the city streets had come to find him. He feared it always would.

Tonight he had gone for a walk. That's what he did when a problem vexed him. He walked to clear his mind and refresh himself. He walked this night out the back tracks over the farmlands, away from civilisation. He walked through Ty Kinsey's land.

Sometimes, just sometimes, it was a quirk of fortune like a left turn over a right turn, like ignoring the word of a crazy old priest or humouring the poor old bastard, that broke a case like this.

****

"Poor Jeffrey. Look at you." Chloe breathed, tears welling at the corners of her eyes. "What did we do to you?"

Jeffrey looked at her, directly at her. "You died," he said simply, his voice a hoarse crackle.

"You can see me?" she cried, her surprise plain.

"Of course I can." He sighed. "I'm dead too, ain't I?"

"I'd hoped you might be able to ... I wasn't sure though. No one else can."

"Well ... they shouldn't," he said.

"Why?" Chloe asked, her brow furrowing.

"Because you're dead. And what's dead should stay that way."

"Yes, I agree now. I'm sorry for ... all this. How do you feel?"

"Worse than I look," Jeffrey replied. There was a little bitterness in his voice. "I should be like you."

"And I'm really sorry for that, Jeff. Really."

"What's done's done. So, what do you want? It's been weeks, Chloe."

"I know. I was too ashamed to come see you," Chloe said, sadness in her voice.

"Better you'd come sooner. Before this," he replied, gesturing to his state.

133

"Better late than never, eh?" Chloe sighed.

"Why now, Chloe. I'm too tired. I need ... I dunno what."

"Tommy and Jade need you, Jeff. They ... they're ..."

"They really don't need this, Chloe."

"Have you seen them lately?"

"They won't answer my calls. And I can't very well go out like this, can I?"

"You need to see them, Jeff. Talk to them."

"How can I? They won't talk to me and I can't go out. How can I help you? What's wrong?"

"They're ... I don't know. They're just in danger. Jade's gonna get killed if we don't do something, Jeff!" Chloe said, panic rising.

"What can I do?" Jeff moaned.

"Call them, and I'll help if I can." Chloe assured him.

His head sank to his chest in resignation. He was bound to help. They were his friends.

****

Leadership and control were new concepts for Jade. She had never assumed such a position in all her life, but it seemed that the world had chosen this moment to test her skill. She saw clearly now what had happened and was sure she knew how to respond. It was almost comically simple when she sat and thought about it.

Tommy's book helped her figure it out. She had gone to it for information on how to do what they had failed in doing as a group, but it had revealed so much more. It spoke of things in the world that she struggled to imagine, forces and feints that were all around and affected her in many miniscule ways. The book and its teaching consumed her totally and revealed the path to her and its reason for being.

When Jade had first appeared in town she had been a different girl. She was happy to follow others, happy to give her body to the great beast pleasure. That's why her father had sent her to this backwater. Because it was far safer for her than a city where she might be totally corrupted in her pursuit of the next high, the next good time. She had brought that same reckless abandon to this town, yet Jeffrey had tempered it. Jeffrey and his friends had made her a better person, one better equipped for life beyond the town. Then Jeffrey had been taken from them; like the world had shown them the way through Jeffrey, now it was giving them a chance.

Chloe had run, in her inability to handle the pressure of self. Tommy had run too, in a more psychological sense. It had been thrust upon her to take control of the situation and handle it she certainly would. She was a stubborn young woman, not one to give in. Tommy had been on the right tracks but a few details had been overlooked. She could rectify his mistakes and get the working totally right with Chloe. She knew because the book had told her so.

She leafed through her tarot and laid her hand on the book while they spoke into her and told her the things she needed to do. She listened to their words and acted upon their wisdom. All the better to ensure her plans were successful.

****

The telephone call was the last straw. The cracked and gurgling voice as dry as the grave would have been bad enough, that the voice was his friend was what tipped Tommy over the edge. Had he received the call before Jade's visit, or a week earlier, then the impact would not have been so terrible. As it was it was the finish of him.

Jeffrey had been his anchor for so long, the voice so soothing to his spirit, that to hear it so reduced was mind breaking.

They had always had a close bond, but when they both lost siblings it drew them closer even than brothers. They had some kind of mutual understanding of each other's pain and knew what it meant to have a brother dead before his time. They had both dealt with their losses in different ways. Jeffrey, the more analytical was philosophical about it; there was nothing to be done about it. Tommy gave vent to his grief by finding an appetite for self-destruction. Once, Tommy had wagered that he could swim across the town water tower. He had discovered a way in and found that it was possible, it was Jeffrey who pointed out what would happen if the tower suddenly went into operation as he swam across. When Jeffrey described how the suction would pull him under and crush him into the pipework, he reconsidered.

There were plenty more times when Tommy had decided on some act of recklessness and his friend was always there to talk him down.

Tommy also had a darker side that Jeffrey did not possess. Once in a while, Tommy would delve into the deepest of depressions and even spoke half-heartedly about suicide. Every year, around the time of his brother's death his mother would be so shattered by grief that she was beyond help, his father would begin to drink far too much and Tommy was left to feel his inadequacy. Would they feel so bad if it had been he who had died? He suspected possibly not. And when those feelings arose, no matter how well he tried to hide his melancholia, Jeffrey was there and just knew. They would walk around and talk alone for hours, or the girls would come along and they would laugh his hurts away.

Those days were gone, he knew that now. Jeffrey and Chloe had gone the way of his brother; Jade was gone too but in a totally different sense. For the first time in his life he felt truly alone.

He had run a gauntlet of emotions in the days and weeks since Jeffrey's death, from anger and hurt at Jeffrey's ingratitude to the thing he felt now, total and utter desolation and self hatred. It had been his idea to attempt the magic that had raised Jeffrey, before that it had been his invitation that had taken Jeffrey out the night he slipped and died, even Chloe had been murdered as a result of his planning and scheming. All paths led back to him and his damned grief.

"We have to talk."

Poor Jeffrey

The voice that was Jeffrey had spoken four words. They were not hard words nor were they uttered with any hint of malice, just a statement or request. Yet the many hells those four words opened up in Tommy's mind were enough. Talk about what? Accusation? Recrimination? He had almost fooled himself into believing that it had all been a bad dream, that it wasn't his doing. The voice, that dry and cracked voice, had brought his fabrications crashing down.

He didn't think. Thinking had caused enough harm already. Jade had assumed that he was unnecessary to her own little scheme, she was mistaken. It all worked on numbers and a certain continuity, even in this chaos. In this case that number and continuity was three. So, unthinking, he took the knife without truly seeing it and drew the blade across his own throat. It bit hungrily and he had applied force enough to slice most of the way through his neck. He lived long enough to see the first gout of blood spray across his desk.

****

In the hours leading up to the biggest event in the town's existence, darkness was flitting in every shadow the harsh sunlight would afford the baking citizens. In darkened bedrooms and shaded groves, people looked over their shoulders and silently, secretly, they plotted escapes.

In truth it had been going on for weeks. Chloe had spotted it during her wanderings around the town as she got used to her new corporeal state. People looked at each other strangely, as though haunted, because that's exactly what they were. They were looking around for the owner of the breath on their neck, the brush on the arm. Every person in the town could feel the very air becoming charged with some unknowable force.

In the suburbs on this day, there were no children playing on the streets or in the municipal park. Their parents wanted to keep them real close, where they could keep a watchful eye on them. In the fields and the factories of the surrounding towns, men called in sick; themselves wanting nothing more than to cuddle up to their wives and children in expectation of some oncoming catastrophe.

In the chapel, Father Cade gave a short-notice sermon all based on the events of the past weeks. He glared from the pulpit as he orated on the dangers of allowing the city to invade their berg, the evils that the city-folk would bring. His favoured theme lately, but this time lent more fire. He tore at his vestments and spittle flew from his lips as his righteous indignation rose as the rhetoric went on. After the service, several of the regular members of the congregation wondered aloud about the good Father's sanity and whether they would return for his next sermon. Several first time worshippers vowed to come to see every sermon from that day on.

In Henrietta's, all eyes turned as Old Man Haggerty walked into the bar and pulled up a seat. Ordering a large measure of liquor, he looked around the room with eyes that could barely have a vision in them and nodded. "Been thinkin' about getting out of this town, Henrietta," he said portentously. "Somethin' just don't feel right."

Nothing would have been strange about this scene, except that Old Haggerty had not been seen in Henrietta's in upward of thirty years. Stranger still the fact that the legendary tee totaller would down a shot of drink so readily. It was a source of some conversation for a little while, before more serious conversation took over.

And all the time the shadows were gathering and flitting in that dark space at the edge of vision, watching and waiting for that deepening darkness ... nightfall.

****

He had wanted to feed that night. It would have been his final meal in town, it would have brought proceedings full circle. He had watched the blonde girl for almost all the two weeks and had decided long ago that she would be with him and she would be the last. She made it very easy.

She was there every evening like clockwork, almost like a secret love tryst where he watched and she luxuriated in the scrutiny. Sometimes she would mutter softly to the shadows like she wanted him to come out of hiding. That night he had watched her with a book and had wanted to take her then, Coltraine would pay for his intervention. He had made the thought, sent the message to his legs to move but they refused. Inside a cold corner of his brain, Coltraine laughed wanly at the small victory.

140

Cal Denver struggled to make his legs move again but nothing would persuade them. Then the girl was leaving and his opportunity was missed.

He sat in Henrietta's now and sipped his beer, smiling and flirting clumsily with the girl who served him his drinks. There was always tomorrow.

****

Sheriff Davies was walking across Kinsey's back field and approaching the rear of the farmhouse when a light breeze drifted over the field. Evening was darkening the sky and all through the walk, the breeze that had brought the sweet aromas of summer with it, now, as he drew closer to the house it brought a much sicklier smell in its folds. It was a smell he'd encountered many times before, but not for years past. Still, after so much time, even the faintest trace of off meat was enough to bring images of violent and messy death to his mind. It brought back thoughts of a young man, chest blown apart. Thoughts of an old lady; unlooked after and uncared for, left to die and rot in her lonely apartment; people caring only when the stench grew unbearable. It brought back memories of such death he almost turned back, unwilling to confront the very nature of terror that he had fled the city in fear of.

As he drew ever closer to the house, he realised that the stench was coming from there. Here was that quirk of fortune. Jeffrey's mother had opened the bedroom window, perhaps to rid the room of the stink. Davies ducked into the shadows, out of sight of the house, and took out his cell phone. He dialled the number of the only man who could help him and it irked the sheriff to call the man greatly as he waited for Frank Fielding to answer.

He started speaking as soon as the line clicked on the other end and the man growled a "Hello?"

"I don't want any questions. Just get as many men as you can muster up to Kinsey's place. Quick about it. We're gonna show these agency pricks how we do things here in the sticks." He hissed into the receiver and immediately hung up without waiting for a response. After a second's thought he made a second call. Better to be safe than sorry.

"Honey," he said, "I might be home a little late."

****

"We need to talk." Jeffrey breathed down the line at the sound of Jade's voice.

"I can't right now, I'm busy," she said, a little too hurriedly.

"We need to talk. Now," he said again; his voice crackly now, like he was underwater.

"Are you okay, Jeff?" Jade asked, though the reply was obvious.

"Been better. You have to come ... come to my ..." He was overcome by a bout of coughs and laboured breathing.

"Really, I can't. Tomorrow."

"Too late. It might be too late tomorrow." Jeffrey breathed heavily now.

"Too late for what? What's going on?"

"You might be in trouble. Just ... come." He sighed.

"Trouble? Have you been speaking to Tommy?" she snapped unintentionally.

"No, Jade. Tommy ... dead," he rattled.

Jade froze at the words, ice right to the core of her. The words were spoken from a voice with such certainty, and with that voice; that awful corpse' rattle. She wanted to disbelieve but knew that Jeffrey wouldn't lie to her, not about this.

"How ... how do you know?" she stammered.

"Come. You have to come. Parents ... out ... come to the barn." Jeff breathed, his strength almost spent.

Jade wanted to deny him, to reply and plead her case, but the line was already dead. It wasn't as if they were so close, she was the new girl. She was more Chloe's friend than Jeffrey's. Why should she go running to him? Her shoulders sagged as she realised her own self-deception. Of course they were friends, from the same circle. When she was new in town, he was among the first kids to offer a friendly word. The last three years had been spent in their company, when she wasn't dragged back to the city with her mother and father. These ties of friendship could not be denied yet she still tried to resist. That was the book talking, the ever encroaching darkness at the edges of her mind.

Now, sitting there holding the dead receiver and the words reverberating in her head, she had no choice.

Poor Jeffrey

****

Foster knew he was probably in trouble. He knew that Neeson coveted his leadership role. He knew that the younger man had ambitions and he had the director's ear. He also knew that the boy was nowhere near experienced enough to take on this case. Luckily, it seemed the director knew it, too.

He walked into the bar with Neeson at his side, knowing that the last phone call Neeson had received was from the boss and that it wasn't the conversation he had expected or wanted. Foster knew because he had received his own phone call to let him know. But he was treading a fine line. They were getting to the point where an arrest must be made or new faces would be brought in. That wouldn't look good for Foster.

He knew that he was a marked man. He had been for some years. The agency had progressed with the times and left Foster standing still. It was no longer his era, it was some future that he would never understand. He was a relic when he was new on the team, now he was defiantly obsolete. He still had skills that were useful. What he did not have was time. He was also irascible, bad tempered and certainly not customer friendly.

The pressure had been ramped up and now Foster was a cornered beast. He would now be tireless in his pursuit of his quarry and he would have to keep his eye on Neeson from now on, too. Neeson's eye was definitely not on the investigation in progress. His thoughts were for what happened after, where his career would lead from this point on. That made him a liability in Foster's eyes.

So, as he went to order his usual drink, bought for show and not for any need of a buzz; he watched Neeson and listened to the bar. Tonight he was close after what he'd heard in previous nights. He was becoming trusted, a part of the furniture and tongues had been loosened. No longer were there suspicious glances and hushed tones when he entered. Now was where the real investigation could begin.

****

Frank Fielding's cell phone rang and was almost missed in the noise inside Henrietta's. Business had picked up and the music was loud in the bar since he had walked in. Fielding didn't often drink in Henrietta's. He much preferred the clubs in the city and would often spend a night or two there, trading business stories with his fellow professionals. He came here now to be with his boys, his workers. He wanted to show them his appreciation for their hard work in the past few weeks and their determination to search for the missing girls *and* make sure his business didn't suffer. He had bought drinks for the night and settled down to have some much deserved downtime.

Jack Coltraine watched the boss man snatch his mobile up and answer it and smile a wicked little smile, a smile that said something had gone his way. Coltraine knew that smile well from other faces; ones he'd seen before and some of that number he'd eaten. Briefly he wondered how the boss man might taste, but he quelled the thought. Such fantasies were dangerous in public. To divert his attention, he watched as Fielding's brow quickly furrowed into a frown. He nodded, his blue eyes turned cold. As whoever it was imparted their message, Frank visibly coiled up like a spring. A few seconds later, he pocketed his phone and nodded at Coltraine and a few other guys who were sat around from his work crew, those few who hadn't drunk too much already. Coltraine had purposely remained sober. The nod was understood and, as one, they all gulped down their drinks and followed their boss out the door.

****

Neeson was still ranting. He was irritating Foster, he had irritated Foster at first sight. He was young, he put all his faith in technology, and now that same technology was failing him and he was lost but wouldn't admit it. Foster was a nose to the stone type of guy, a real field agent with real know how about him, and he was being made to babysit a loser. He wasn't fooling himself into thinking that he could lead the case any better, be any closer to a suspect. But he wouldn't have alienated himself from the locals as Neeson had done so comprehensively. Damn stupid college kid.

He had hoped to find some peace at Henrietta's, maybe even forge a friendship or two between his bouts of surreptitious surveillance. The hope was dashed when Neeson arrived and proceeded to bellyache some more. Foster pretended to listen, nodding in what he guessed might be the appropriate places, but all the time he was watching the bar. He watched the comings and goings, the good humoured greetings and fond farewells. There was a palpable stiffness, a sense of a community trying to paint over the cracks in its façade of bonhomie; each man eyeing the next to see if this neighbour or that lifelong friend had invited the canker in.

Foster was contemplating the sadness and familiarity of the scene when it happened all at once. Across the bar a group of at least ten men, all guys he recognised from Fielding's search parties, rose as one and headed for the door. It didn't look good. Quickly he downed his own drink and grabbed his coat, making for the door himself. Neeson followed, aggravatingly close on his heels.

"What's wrong? Foster! Foster!" cried Neeson at Foster's back.

"Follow me if you got the balls, son." Foster growled without turning. "I do believe we're gonna have to stop a lynching."

****

Chloe went to check on Tommy right after Jeffrey had replaced the receiver. She had a cold feeling as soon as he turned to her and sighed. In time she would learn how to travel at the speed of thought, but not yet. This time she was too late; the bedroom wall was already soaked, his desk the same. Tommy's body was on the chair, head tipped back too far and blood pumping lazily into his shirt, turning white cotton to deep crimson.

"I didn't know a body had so much blood inside," Tommy said from the edge of the bed where he sat.

"What did you do?" Chloe gasped as she turned to look at him.

"I couldn't handle it anymore. Everything was a reminder; everything was ... telling me it was my fault. Then Jade ..."

"I was watching you. You were so sad."

"Stupid, not sad. That book ... those feelings ... anyway ... done now." Tommy sighed.

"It's not done, Tommy. Jeffrey still needs our help. You know that, right?"

"Yeah. I thought we might've ... you know?" Tommy said, his hands motioning the departure of himself.

"I know ... "

"Jade is gonna try the working again. Did you see that?" Tommy asked.

"I know. We have to help her, Tom."

"She won't listen. She's into it now. Addicted."

"It's not just the book and the magic, Tom. The guy who killed me, he's been watching her," Chloe said.

"Really? She's gone crazy, you know?" Tommy replied.

"Not crazy. She's just confused. Right now, we have to go to Jeffrey."

148

"Yeah. I thought I'd have to go see him when I didn't go poof."

He sighed and got up from the bed. He hadn't taken his eyes from his own remains since Chloe had walked in, now he looked right at her and smiled. When her eyes met his she saw that old light was back. He seemed almost happy again. Almost.

****

Sheriff Davies had moved position so he could watch the front and rear of the house and hunkered down in the shadows. He badly wanted a cigarette; waiting had never been something he'd enjoyed. Soon, he hoped to hear the roar of engines.

His legs started to burn and his knees popped when he tried to stand and stretch, so much so that he nearly fell when the back door of the house was opened. His heart almost stopped when he saw the figure that staggered like a drunk across the yard, the arms too long for the torso and the legs too short.

Sheriff Davies knew that shape; he had watched it grow into the shape it was. Davies was the guy who had scraped those remains off the road. It wasn't possible. Yet here he was, seeing it with his own eyes, smelling it with his own nose. The sight of Jeffrey Kinsey, dead yet walking, turned his bowels to water. Sudden sweat sprang cold from his brow and made him shake from head to foot. He had seen many things in his time as a city cop, but never had he seen a dead kid walk. He wanted to run, wanted to make a call, but all he could do was watch, his heart beating madly in its cage. As Jeffrey shambled into the barn, Sheriff Davies looked down and saw a wet patch blossoming on the front of his trousers. He sank into a crouch and started to weep.

He had waited in the hope of catching a killer. Never had he expected to see a corpse walk. The seeing almost unhinged him.

****

Jade was questioning the wisdom of venturing out. The book called to her, impatient to be used, and her hands itched for its proximity. Over the few short hours the book had been in her care, its will had invaded her mind and taken hold. There was no returning from the course it had set for her. Like a forbidden lover, Jade would have to accede to its demands and, like a lover, it would take full advantage of her weakness.

Yet Jeffrey's invitation could not be denied. Impatient and irritated with circumstances as she was and as preoccupied as she was by her research, she knew she couldn't avoid meeting Jeffrey, especially considering that what she was planning was in part for him. The memory of his kindnesses and the reason for her mission far outweighed her need to look at the book ... for now, at least.

As she turned into the gateway of Kinsey's farm, she heard the sound of engines being pushed to their limits and the screeching of tyres. Perhaps Troy Pinder and Paul Garratty were racing their new cars again, a little of the city creeping into the small town was disappointing to Jade.

She walked on up the driveway, not giving the sound another thought. If the boys wanted to wrap themselves around a tree it was none of her concern. Her concentration was on the barn, the meeting place. She wondered if she was late.

****

Frank Fielding strode out of Henrietta's, his men like hounds on his heels. He barked orders at them, giving only the vaguest notion of what they were racing toward. He mentioned that the killer may be about to get caught and that Sheriff Davies was alone at the Kinsey farm. That was enough for the boys. Fielding smiled a little as two trucks full of working men followed his own truck out of town. He liked the feeling of power the situation gave him. Davies had called him, *him* of all people. That must've hurt the old crone's pride.

Fielding gunned the engine until it whined, taking the bends at speeds bordering on suicidal. He remembered times in his youth when truck pursuits like these were common. When he was in his teens there had been several years of feuding between a couple of the farmers around the town. Frank's father had been asked, along with the mayor, to act as adjutants in the feuds and attempt a peaceful resolution. As

151

so often was the case in small towns, the resentments ran deep and any resolutions or promises were broken. So the two gangs of farm workers would often fight in the bar and every so often there would be some act of vandalism or some sleight that would warrant a visit to their opponent's farm for a dust up. The young men, like Frank, had followed these convoys of trucks, if only to see the fist fight that would ensue. Very occasionally, weapons were drawn and shots fired. That was when, almost like a ghost, Sheriff Denbrooke would show up and bust a few skulls. He was a mountain of a man and he wasn't afraid of being in the thick of the battle, unlike his current successor. Fielding smiled at the memory as he negotiated the country bends at speeds he hadn't driven at for well over two decades. If he were honest, Frank Fielding might even say he was enjoying himself.

For Coltraine and the boys, the ride to Kinsey's farm was exhilarating in the back of the flatbed as Frank Fielding threw the vehicle into the bends and gunned the engine furiously when the roads straightened. Cal/Jack sat and waited with anticipation.

Fielding had explained in vague terms what they were racing toward and he watched the other men as they primed their pistols and even one or two rifles. It had unnerved him a little how readily the small arsenal of weapons had appeared by their sides as if from nowhere. In movies and fictions were small towns always shown this way. He had never imagined those fantasies to be true, yet as he sat and watched the eyes of the men opposite and alongside him, he quickly realised that their words of bravado and promises of retribution uttered at the beginning of the searches were exactly that, promises.

These were blood hungry men on the hunt, they were dangerous. He saw murder in each pair of eyes. Cal Denver, however, did not feel fraternity in their company now. He was afraid of what their thirst might lead to.

****

The barn was lit with a sickly glow from the oil lamps which hung at intervals along the rafters of the hay loft. Jeffrey sat on an aged chair in the centre of the space. Jade fell apart as soon as her eyes alighted on him. In her dreams she had seen him restored and whole, she had seen her circle of friends together again. In the real world, miracles did not happen; she realised that when her friend raised his head and his gummy, rheumy eyes met her sparkling, tear-blurred blue ones.

Oh, but he looked so tortured. She wanted to go over and hold him, to soothe his considerable hurts but he looked so fragile, so utterly corrupted that the slightest touch might unmake him. The stink of him almost made her gag.

"You came," he wheezed in surprise. "Thank you."

"You sounded awful ... on the phone," she replied, weakly.

"A lot's happened, Jade. Too much." He sighed.

"I thought we could put it right ..." she began.

"No one could, Jade. Not ... possible," Jeffrey said,

153

attempting to put force in his words and failing.

"When you left … we were lost, Jeff," she began to sob at the admission.

"Tell her what you saw," Tommy called from the shadows. Jade gasped as he unknitted from the gloom with Chloe at his side.

"I can see you, Tommy," she gasped.

"You can? Really?" Chloe asked in surprise.

"It's not a surprise." Tommy laughed. "All the shit she's been doing? Of course she can see us."

"Why? Am I going crazy?" Jade asked, her unease growing.

"Crazy? No. But the stuff you've been messing with is bad news, Jade. It gets inside and opens your mind, messes you up. Gotta get rid of it, babe. It ain't for you," Tommy warned.

"But then … how can I fix this? Where did the working go wrong? Why did you all have to leave me?" Jade sobbed, her voice becoming more shrill. She looked like a little girl.

"It isn't meant to be fixed, Jade. It doesn't work that way," Jeffrey said.

"The magic worked perfectly. You know that," Chloe went on.

"Shit happens. Like my brother dying and Jeff's … you just gotta get on, babe. What's dead's gotta stay dead," Tommy finished.

"Out of time." Jeffrey sighed, his head sinking to his chest. "Cars."

"Shit," Tommy hissed.

"What?" Jade asked in some confusion.

"We need to get Jeff outta here," Tommy said urgently.

"Why? What's happening?" Jade asked again.

"The good ole' boys are coming," Chloe groaned.

****

Klimpt Davies had watched in horror as Jade wandered into Kinsey's yard and into the barn after the apparition. He felt a coward for not going after her, but he had seen what was inside.

Did she not know what the boy was? Did she even know that he was there? She must know, surely? He had seen and disbelieved his own eyes at first, but time had planted certainty in his marrow. Jeffrey Kinsey was the walking dead! It was he who was responsible for the killings, he who must have eaten those poor girls alive. One of the girls had been close to him, too. That thought sent shards of ice down his spine. Where the hell were Frank's boys? Davies lay, rooted in the shadows, and prayed they wouldn't be too late. Just in case they were, he made one last call. This one to Father Cade. After all, if he couldn't save Jade Cole he could at least attempt to save his own soul.

****

Deputy Barrett and the men were not on their way to their

sheriff's aid, they hadn't even received his message. They were with Tommy's mother, consoling her after her grizzly discovery.

Barrett sat on the porch step rubbing his eyes, trying to erase the image of the boy's head tipped back so very far; the blood spatter on the wall and the bloody blade by the boy's hand. He shook his head, perhaps he might shake the silent movie out of his skull. Barrett had seen far too much death during the past weeks, too many opened torsos and leaking veins. He was just a small town deputy and this wasn't what he signed up for. He had expected to sign a few traffic violations, perhaps put a drunk or two in the jail to cool off every now and then. Violent death and gore was not in the job description for him. He wanted to be able to lie at night and sleep sound dreams, not jump at every little sound in the house in case it may be the killer come to take his own daughter. He was considering a career change; he was considering a total life change at that moment. Had he been at the Kinsey farm that night, he might have gone completely mad.

As it was, by the end of the week he was leading an exodus.

****

The truck slid around the corner, through the gateway and up the driveway, kicking up dust and stones in its wake. Sheriff Davies came out of hiding, hands waving and face white with worry and shock. Fielding stamped on the brakes and brought the truck to a skidding halt. The sheriff looked to see the fifteen men, all armed and jumping down from the trucks. The sight gave the sheriff a moment of relief.

"What do we got, Sheriff?" Fielding growled. As he stepped from the cab and slung his own rifle over his shoulder, he looked down in some disdain at the sheriff's wet crotch.

"The murderer, Frank. We got our fucking killer!" hissed Davies.

"You're sure?" Fielding said, eyes narrowing and moving in the direction Davies was pointing. "Where?"

"In the barn ... but ..."

The sheriff's words were lost as Fielding motioned to the men and, as one, they followed their boss in his purposeful march to the barn in a din of clicking weapons and hollering.

Frank walked ahead of his men and pointed to the left and the right of him, the men responded instantly, surrounding the barn and making sure that there would be no escape. They whooped and hollered as they went, excited at the prospect of what was to come. Frank simply strode with an even and steady gait to the doors, like an executioner. He looked over his shoulder; there were five men around him, including the sheriff. He glanced down at the man with a look of immense distaste, then he opened the door and went inside.

****

"What the hell do you mean you're stayin'" Tommy yelled incredulously.

"No ... time." Jeffrey sighed, shaking his head. "Tell Jade, Tommy."

"Tell Jade what?" Jade shouted as the vehicle outside skidded to a halt.

"You can't just stay, Jeff!" Tommy yelled.

"Tommy! Tell me!" Jade pleaded.

"You're in danger, Jade ..." Chloe began.

"I know that, you said ... the book," Jade snapped.

"No. Not the book," Chloe said. "The guy who killed me, he's watching you now."

"What?" Jade gasped. "How do you know?"

"I watched him. I can feel him and I think he can kinda feel me, too. He ate me, you see? He wants to eat you, too," Chloe warned.

"But how ... I mean, I haven't been anywhere! Who is he?"

"He watches you in the graveyard. He's not anyone we know," Chloe said.

"So, what does he look like? We can tell the sheriff and ..."

"And what? You gonna tell em a ghost told ya?" Tommy said.

"I could say I saw him in the graveyard."

"No. We have a plan, but we need to get Jeff outta here," Tommy said.

"I'm ... not leaving." Jeffrey sighed.

"Jeff! The sheriff is gonna think ..."

"I know what the sheriff thinks, Tommy," Jeffrey replied weakly. "I'm banking on it."

"What? What does that mean? We gotta go, man."

"Too ... late." Jeffrey sighed, his eyes on the door.

****

He watched the others split off into groups and surround the building, waiting in their positions after they'd shouted themselves hoarse with their initial whooping and caterwauling. No words were spoken and no signal given at all as far as he could tell, they just seemed to know instinctively what needed to be done. He was impressed; he hadn't believed such simpletons capable of cohesion so close to perfection. Nothing in his time with these people had they shown such capability, even parts of the searches had bordered on farce at times. He followed them a little way; on one hand eager to see the operation to completion, on the other needing to be seen to be with the mob when the final act was under way in case suspicion fell on him next. After a short time watching, he darted away unseen into the shadows.

Now he stood by Fielding's truck and watched in mild amusement as, at some order or call he couldn't hear, each one of the townsmen disappeared into the barn.

****

He trudged through the town and out the opposite side from the church in a hurry. This was one of those times that Father Cade wished he still had his car. The phone call from Sheriff Davies had shaken him, no more than a few hurried words but more than enough to spring him in to action. He had laced his shoes and run out the door in moments, Exodus the dog close behind.

Now he ran up the lane in a sweat, wondering what it was that he might find up at Kinsey's farm. As he came closer to the land, he heard a cacophony of men rising up from the farmhouse, it seemed to him. The noise lent his heels extra speed, though his breath burned hot in his chest and his heart was beating against his chest wildly. He had to get up there and see what was happening and if the Kinsey's were safe. At that moment his worst fear was to find Marie and Tyrone Kinsey hanging from a tree.

He came to the gateway and ran up the deeply rutted and dusty track, his eyes locked on the house. The squat, clapboard farmhouse looked deserted, its windows all dark. He looked across at the outbuilding but that too seemed utterly deserted. He ran on, passed Frank Fielding's truck and almost bumped right into the man standing there; watching something that was happening further on, beyond the house.

"Who are you?" panted the Father.

"Just watching for the boys, Father," the man replied, scratching the stubble at his cheek.

"What's happening?" the old priest snapped.

"Dunno," the man replied without looking at him. "Frank

and the boys seemed awful excited though. Go take a look if you want."

"Yes ... maybe I will."

Cal had fallen into the Coltraine persona as soon as he saw the old priest running up the track and was completely prepared for what he would say when the old man had got to his side and followed his gaze up the hill. During the short exchange he had watched the old man's every movement, trying to work out if he had any fight in him or if he was a victim. He had never had cause to speak to the priest, but he had heard about the old man's crazy sermons about the city being hell on earth. Insanity was perhaps the only thing that scared Cal Denver, it was too unpredictable.

As the priest spoke, he thought about what to do about him. He couldn't allow the man to simply walk away; he had seen his face and spoken with him. On this night that couldn't be allowed to pass. He wondered how the man would taste. If he had the time he might have liked to make a meal of the old priest, if only to see if his position made his meat taste any sweeter.

"Maybe I will ..." the priest had said and made off further up the track toward the barn. Cal made his snap decision and followed smartly on his heels. His eyes quickly scanned the horizon and confirmed what he already knew from his instinct, he was not being watched. He turned his attention back to the priest. In his haste he hadn't noticed that he was being followed. He made this so simple.

Denver kicked the old man's legs from beneath him a

little more forcefully than was necessary. He winced as he heard bones crack when the man fell. Quickly, before he could make much noise, Cal bent over the man and bit into his neck with all the force he could muster and tore out a large portion of the side of the man's turkey-skinned throat. Blood spouted from the wound and splashed over Cal's face. He licked his lips and went to suckle at the crimson fountain. The old man struggled a little, but Cal held him down; the frailty of the priest was no match for Cal's strength. All too soon the fight went out of him completely and he lay still, his heart stopped.

Cal Denver was disappointed; he had hoped that there would be something special in the priest's meat. He had hoped for some kind of redemption perhaps. Yet here he stood, over the body of a broken old crone, still as unsatisfied as ever. The meat tasted no sweeter for all its godliness.

He picked up the priest's body and threw it into the field by the side of the track, wiped off his bloodstained face and went back to his post by the truck. He hoped for a main course to compliment his unexpected appetiser.

****

"What in the name of ..." Frank Fielding gasped in horror. He had burst into the barn expecting any number of lunacies, what confronted him now almost turned his bowels to water. He had stood on the edge of Jeffrey Kinsey's grave and thrown in dirt; he had looked into his casket at the funeral

162

and paid his respects along with the others. He looked nothing like the monstrosity that stood before him now that was so undeniably Jeffrey Kinsey; his skin gangrenous and peeling to reveal dry muscle underneath, pieces of grey skull peeking through his scalp. For a second Fielding was floundering at the sight until sense flooded into him and he understood that what he was seeing was some kind of disguise. Surely this was simply a vagrant in his rags. Then he saw the girl, tears streaking her face and anger flared within him. With anger came words. "What the fuck do you think you're doing, scumbag. Come over here now, honey. You're safe now."

No ... don't ... he isn't ..." Jade stammered.

"Just ... go." Jeffrey breathed, his words almost lost amid the din of men's boots and exclamations.

Jade looked back at her friend as she turned to leave and a sob escaped her.

"You killed them poor girls didn'tcha, scumball?" Fielding leered.

"No," Jeffrey wheezed, watching Jade push her way between the group of townsmen.

"Oh but you did, ungodly piece of filth that you are," Fielding yelled.

"You ... know me, Frank. I wouldn't do that." Jeffrey breathed, holding Fielding's glare.

"Don't you speak to me, boy. I don't know shit about whom or what the fuck you are." Fielding growled.

"I'm not gonna ... argue, Frankie ... If you think I'm the

163

one … then do what you gotta do …" Jeffrey stammered, barely able to see straight but still holding Fielding's stare defiantly.

"What do we do with it, boss? It fucking stinks," a man in the group gagged.

"It can't live. No one would believe it ..." Sheriff Davies began.

"Shut up, Davies. This is town business now. You know what that means, boy?" Fielding growled. His decision had been made.

Jeffrey nodded, understanding what the look in Fielding's eyes meant, and slowly stood, spreading his arms out wide. "Thank … you," he wheezed.

Unseen by the men, Tommy and Chloe placed their arms around him.

****

Jade stumbled past the leering and grimacing faces that were a blur of ugliness and out into the yard. She heard the threats and she wanted to hear no more. It had taken her too long to realise what she and her friends had done. What more harm they could have done had they carried on as she had planned? The death of Chloe was the least of it all; perhaps the killer would get away because of this diversion. So many things had happened as a result of their dabbling in forces that none of them understood. The realisation had killed Tommy. She had to put that right.

Jade stumbled away from the barn and down the track. She knew where she needed to go. She saw the truck at the bottom of the yard. There was someone waiting out there somewhere wanting her dead. She stumbled on as shots were fired, sounding too loud in her ears. Tears blurred her vision and another sob escaped her, the significance of the sound not lost on her.

"It's what was right, no matter how it happened, you know that, right?" said Jeffrey, suddenly at her side and smiling down at her with that crooked grin of his.

Tommy and Chloe were with him, just like always. Jade smiled at the rightness of it.

"I know. But you're going to leave me now." Jade sighed.

"We won't. We got stuff still to do." Tommy winked.

"Right now, the guy's here. You know what to do, Jade?" Chloe asked, concern on her face.

"Just act like nothin's wrong, let him do what he needs to do and we'll do the rest. Don't get so scared, Jade, we're right here," said Tommy.

"By your side all the time," whispered Jeffrey.

Jade nodded and stumbled on down the track a few steps toward the truck. Her friends went with her, standing either side of her like an invisible barrier. She didn't see where the killer was, neither did she want to. The less she knew, the better her act of compliance would be. She felt comforted by her friends' proximity then she felt nothing at all as the blow came down.

Poor Jeffrey

****

The townsmen acted quickly after the shooting. As one they moved to throw the oil lamps into the hay loft. The fire took hungrily in the dry straw and soon the barn was ablaze. Not content with the destruction, they moved to the house with torches and burned that, too. The Kinsey's would not be coming home. The town had decided. They watched the house burn to cinders and ash, only then did anyone call the firehouse. The cover up had already begun. As in small towns all across the world, this would be the town's dirty secret. There would be a rational explanation for the Kinsey house burning down; there were whispers of it already among the men. By morning the version of events that were cooked up in those moments were written into history and for years to come there would be fireside tales of the night the Kinsey's left town.

"What a tragedy that Ty Kinsey, in his grief, had left those oil lamps burning when he'd gone out," they would say. "Such a shame."

****

Foster was driving quickly, but taking no risks on these dusty roads and had lost Fielding's truck. The whole endgame at the barn must have taken only moments to play out. As he rounded the last bend, he saw a pall of black smoke beginning to rise from the Kinsey farm. Too late. Neeson had

166

begun to breathe heavily in the seat beside him; his face turned pallid and seat beaded on his upper lip. He wasn't going to be much use if it came to confrontation.

Fucking desk jockey.

He was about to turn into the track when Fielding's flatbed roared out of the gateway, almost colliding with them. In the glare of headlights he saw the pallid face of a man he recognised from the searches, beside him was Jade Cole; terror etched across her face and her mouth gagged. "No fucking way," Foster growled as he spun the car in the gateway and gave chase. He wouldn't drive so carefully this time. Because as Sheriff Davies also believed, sometimes a quirk of luck like this broke a case.

****

Cal Denver drove like a maniac back toward the town. It was fortuitous that his girl had run right into his arms. It was almost like she had expected and welcomed her abduction as she walked so calmly to the truck. He waited until she came alongside the driver's door and simply struck her in the head. She did not cry out, simply crumpled into his arms under the force of the blow. He regretted having to strike her but he couldn't risk her crying out. It was fortuitous also that Fielding had left the keys for his truck in the ignition. To Cal Denver it seemed almost like he was being aided in his pursuit somehow. He smiled as he gripped the wheel. He had hoped that the scene at the barn might have offered some revelation; it had disappointed him to witness such wanton destruction. Time to move on then. In search of revelation … or just sweeter meat.

Jade struggled a little in the seat. He'd bound her quickly and been off and away but she hadn't remained unconscious for long. He stroked her hair and hushed her, smiling down at her. Time to close the circle.

****

The world knows magic and dark deeds will respond accordingly. It remembers. The world speaks and acts in ways unseen and unknowable, yet it does act. Sometimes when a great man falls, the world mourns and puts forth rich shoots where he has lain, because resurrection is beyond even her power. When the darkest of deeds are done, the world shuns the part of its flesh which bore the act. Some places it feels like the world is holding its breath, waiting.

On occasion the world will rebel. The effects of her actions might not be felt by mere human beings, but they are shown. Subtle vibrations and waves of pure will summon her allies to her side on these occasions. Sometimes, she rebels.

****

Cal Denver smiled when he looked in the mirror and saw no headlights or silhouetted movements following them. He swung the truck into a small yard and killed the engine, whistling tunelessly as he walked around the truck. Jack was all but gone now, it didn't take long once the pills had run out. There would be no tears, no apologies, just sated hunger. He opened the door and dragged the girl out, slamming the door shut behind him, and walked to his chosen ground.

She struggled, but only a little. Just enough for her pride to tell her she'd at least tried.

He marched her into the shadows of the chapel and enjoyed the sound of her groaning when she realised where they were. He shoved her in the back, leading her to the place where he'd watched a body interred weeks earlier then watched her and her friends raise it again. He had watched in horror, and no small admiration, as the corpse had pulled itself out of its grave. It had led to a frenzy of hunger and Cal's release.

All the time in a corner of his mind, totally unnoticed by Cal, was a small gnawing. Some tiny voice spoke about the world and its memory or some such superstition. Sometimes, the voice that was Jack Coltraine and sometimes not brought tears and pain, it brought a heart bursting with regret. Now it was almost silent, surely victory was Denver's now. Had Cal heard and heeded that voice, he might not have so enjoyed the perversity of his final act in this town. If he saw the agitation in the trees, in the ground, he wouldn't feel so satisfied with his last message to the people of this town.

He would have run for his life.

Closing circles make a huge bang.

Poor Jeffrey

****

Foster drove into town and by some sheer luck, he spotted the truck in the graveyard, dust still rising around it from its sudden stop. He smiled as he swung into the tight parking area and stopped his vehicle behind the already parked truck. He looked over and checked Neeson. He was checking his pistol for the umpteenth time, shaking fingers struggling to slide the bullets back into their chamber. Foster laid his hand lightly over the young man's, as much to curb his irritation as to offer comfort.

"Are you gonna be okay, Tim? I'm gonna need you to be solid," Foster warned, looking into the pallid face of Neeson.

"I will be as professional as ever." Neeson smiled wanly.

"You'll back me the fuck up, or I'll shoot you myself." Foster growled. "Now come on, if we're not already too late we have a young girl's life to save."

He stepped out of the confines of the truck and breathed in the fresher air, fingers moving over his own weapon on instinct, checking the bullets were there and that the safety catch was off. He took a moment to steady his own nerves then moved around the truck and into the shadow of the church, an audibly trembling Neeson following on his heels.

Neeson watched the graveyard unfold over Foster's shoulder. He fought to hold down the contents of his stomach as little by little his nerves got the better of him. He had been in situations like this one had the potential to become, but back then he'd had twenty men around him and

170

sniper squads. Never in his short career had he been in a situation like this without back up. In his training this was the kind of situation they always advised against. Had he known, when Foster grabbed his coat and run out of Henrietta's, what Foster had in mind then he would certainly have protested, called for back-up and done things the right way; the procedural way. But had he done that, would they be so close to the killer that Foster had trailed for so very long? He was beginning to doubt it. Had things been done his way then likely all they would have found was another body, eaten away and torn apart. It made him cold inside to consider what his attitude may have cost them had Foster said anything. Yet even now he questioned the wisdom of what they were about to do. He stepped in Foster's footsteps on leaden feet, his legs shaking under the strain of indecision; should they stay and see out this act or run as fast as they could away from this lunacy?

Foster sensed the turmoil in Neeson. To a veteran agent like Del Foster it stank like manure. He half turned and checked his partner over, looking him right in the eye. It was a look that told the younger man what the consequences of flight would be. Once assured that Neeson would be behind him, he rounded the corner of the chapel and then bolted across the small patch of lawn to a stand of shrubbery. Once there, if he craned his neck he could see the killer silhouetted in the moonlight with Jade Cole held out before him.

Foster recognised the spot instantly. It was the Kinsey grave. He had been shown the scene by the cops; believing it to have some kind of connection with the murders, at least those from town. He had ruled out that idea and here was the proof of his error. His heart fluttered at the proximity between him and the killer. For so long he had dreamed of this moment and now, here it was. He took a step around the bushes, hoping that the shadows would be enough to conceal him. He risked a quick glance at Neeson and was given scant reassurance by the wreck he had become. It didn't matter now what kind of man Neeson would prove himself to be. The endgame was now in play.

He took another step closer to the scene unfolding before him, then another. When he had time to think about it, he would appreciate the metaphor in these final acts. Step by step he had closed on the killer. And here, step by step …

****

Jade had to fight against every instinct in her fibre to remain submissive to the man who pushed her toward Jeffrey's grave. It was her deepest wish that she could turn and fight this animal, but that was not the plan. She tried to let her mind go blank, to escape the situation that she was in, but it was no good. His voice spoke softly in her ear and brought her back to the reality of the moment.

She tried to look around, to see where her friends had taken up their positions but it was no good, her captor would not allow her to look over her shoulder. He didn't seem much troubled by her constant searches, his belief was that

172

no one was coming.

He pushed her on to the patch of ground that had once held Jeffrey and smiled at her warmly. His cordial demeanour made her angry enough to lash out at him, until she remembered herself and calmed her temper. "You'll be safe inside me," he kept saying, over and over. The words made her feel sick.

After a little while of looking at her, reassuring her, he stepped behind her and allowed her to look out over the graveyard. She could see her friends looking on, concentrating on their task. In the shadows of the chapel she saw the shapes of two men approaching. In the gloom of the trees and the bushes she saw other shapes and agitations darting around, too quick for her eyes to make sense of what she saw. It was enough for her to know that she wasn't alone. She was calmer now than she ever was. She could smell the man behind her, a mix of sweat, fire and desperation. She could see her friends there. She focused on the group and waited for whatever was going to happen.

****

"Son of a bitch!" Jeffrey yelled. "That's the guy who killed me!"

"What?" Tommy exclaimed. "Are you sure, dude?"

"I'm sure. He had a beard then, but it's definitely him," Jeffrey growled. "And I felt sorry for him?"

"Relax," Chloe said. "We have to be calm. Concentrate."

What they were attempting would be possible if they had more practice. To touch, to feel. To pick up a stone and throw it. They might do all of that and more given time to learn. Time they did not have, so they called for help. Just as they felt the world doing.

They only needed the will.

Yet concentration was difficult with Jade being led to her death right there in front of them. It was a part of the plan, but it was still uncomfortable to watch. They could see her being made to kneel at the foot of Jeffrey's grave. Jeffrey closed his eyes, hoping it would be easier to concentrate if he couldn't see. Each spirit thought hard about the vibrations in the ground, the disturbance in the trees and lent their will to the effort.

Then, just as their concentration reached a zenith, two men crashed through them. The feeling was like having a hot blade pushed through them and for a second all that they could see was the men's minds. Chloe screamed at the invasion. Tommy and Jeffrey fought hard to regain their equilibrium.

When their vision cleared they saw that, regardless of their actions, many others were watching now. They had heard the call.

****

Cal stood over Jade as she trembled at his feet, taking a second to savour the sensation of power. He bent her neck as he had so many times and ran his fingers down the smooth flesh of her throat, oh so lightly. Smiling he put his lips to her vein.

"Don't you fucking dare!" shouted the man. "FBI, step away from the girl."

Foster had closed the gap and could look the man right in the face. Recognition sent cold ice shards down his spine and almost made him sick. There, his head mere inches from Jade Cole's jugular, was Jack Coltraine! He was the one that had had his picture printed in papers the country over, the one who had been interviewed by the prettiest young journalists the networks could find. He was the one who had been on the hunts and found the young mute girl, Clare. All these thoughts raced through Foster's mind as his eyes met those of Coltraine. He had been right, this was no lunatic, this man had reason in spades. The gleam in his eye, the slight smile as he gazed down the barrel of Foster's weapon. Here was a man calculating his chances and wondering if there was a way out of the situation he had found himself in.

Cal Denver sighed, his shoulders sagged. He was caught. How had that happened? Many thoughts and fears flashed through his mind all at once, thoughts of incarceration and vilification, accusation and hatred. Death.

"I said step away," the man's voice warned.

The girl trembled beneath his grip. Surely the rightness of this moment should have been noted by these men, surely they should be more reverent. He heard the men's steps, they were advancing on him but nervously. The muscles in his

175

jaws bunched up, ready to champ down.

Neeson watched all this from behind strangely blurred eyes. Fear had given him tunnel vision, it seemed. In his periphery all he could see was mist, but Coltraine was highlighted in crystal clarity. He heard Foster's warnings as if from across a field on a windy day, the words were there but the sense of them lost. His fear had, along with the tunnel vision, given him foresight. He watched Coltraine's eyes, he saw the muscles in his jaw tighten. In his mind he saw blood spurt from the corner of the man's mouth as he took his first bite. The mere suggestion broke him. He stepped in front of Foster and raised his gun, aiming at the side of Coltraine's head. He took a second, watching a small smile play about the killer's eyes. Coldly, he calculated the shot and figured he wouldn't hurt the girl then emptied the gun into the head of Jack Coltraine. The job done, he silently lost his mind.

Then all hell broke loose.

****

More souls had gathered than Tommy, Chloe, or Jeffrey could count. Some were recognisable as the people they had been in life. Tommy could've sworn he had seen the missing girls from town in the throng. Others, those whose anger had overcome their spirit, appeared bestial; still more appeared shapeless and devoid of form, swirling and shifting in the darkness. The malice that exuded from them was overwhelming yet some kind of force held them at a distance.

The throng grew agitated when the men with guns started their advance, perhaps the spirits wanted to see a bullet in the man's brain.

Some of the spirits jumped up and down, gibbering in insane fashion. Most just watched coldly as the warnings were shouted out and summarily ignored. In the trees, some of the ghouls shook the branches as they yelled and hollered.

Then, something changed. The demeanour of the killer had tightened up and gained an almost resolute posture. The older man still shouted out warnings as he approached but too slowly, much too slowly.

The muscles in the man's jaw tightened, the older man's finger squeezed the trigger and the bullet flew; the throng of dark angels moved as one toward the killer and Chloe screamed in terror as she foresaw the outcome of the acts.

Somewhere between the squeezing of the trigger and the man's decision to bite down on his meal, the spirits decided they had seen enough and began to move. The quickest and more eager of the number, the angriest, covered the distance between the trees and the killer in a beat, long before the bullet had chance to do any damage. The man's eyes widened as he seemed to see the forms that were bearing down on him. He raised his head slightly and threw the girl away from him. He still stood with head cocked, a curious little smile on his lips. He regarded the growing crowd of spirits with a mixture of interest and unease … then they made their move.

The spirits hit the killer and he flew, but they did not let him fall. As he flew through the air, the shapeless spirits caught him and held him fast while still more buffeted him and clawed at him. The man shrieked as wounds opened up on his face and his clothes went to shreds to reveal the pink flesh beneath. The spirits only moved quicker in their vengeful violence. His skin was ripped and torn; his shrieks became higher and higher in pitch under the terrible assault of unseen hands.

The agents backed away, the older one taking the younger by the arm; heads shaking in horror and disbelief. Jade curled up in a ball and added her voice to the shrieking of her would-be killer. Then, like a plaster being removed from a wound, the man's flesh was torn away in a shower of blood but still the spirits tore and gouged at the meat and bone of him; a cloud of red hanging in the darkness.

When his head finally sagged and he expired, those who could see watched Cal Denver's dark spirit being torn from the rags of its body. He didn't have time to fear anything, and Tommy doubted he even knew the assault had continued beyond death as the spirits tore his spirit to ever smaller ragged pieces and bloody scraps. On and on the violence continued until there was no trace of his body, not even a smear of blood remained.

Those who were innocent suffered not a scratch.

****

Nothing could be the same around town following the events of those two weeks, and it wasn't. Everything changed.

178

Tyrone and Marie Kinsey didn't return for the sale of their farm. They stayed with the sister they had been visiting the night the farm burned. They never spoke of the loss they'd suffered twice, once by the road and once by the fire. In their dreams though they still walked those fields and watched their sons chasing each other through the long grass. They dreamed of heaven.

One by one, all the folks that had anything to do with the Kinsey fire left town. They never uttered a word of what they had seen that night and yet if anyone had bothered to check, they would find an interesting anomaly. Of those that had been there, all but one had killed themselves within the year; Frank Fielding was the first to go. He got his wish and was indeed elected as town mayor yet the responsibility of office proved too much for him. When he saw the town coffers and the cash that flowed into the town as a result of the murders and media presence he put a hole in his head. His lies had covered up the whole story, it was his grin that had looked out from the front page of the newspapers alongside the good sheriff, and that had brought tourists flocking to see the place where the dastardly endgame had taken place. Only Sheriff Davies was too stubborn not to put a bullet in his own head. As world weary as he was he just couldn't bring himself to pull the trigger that one last time.

It was a ghost town now; all the reporters and cameras were long gone, quickly followed by the townsfolk.

Tim Neeson was led out of the grave yard that early morning. His statement was taken and he was checked into the state sanitarium that same day. Of course Foster's account of the events of the previous evening were quite different to Neeson's own. It had to be.

Neeson's ordered, logic–based psyche had taken too much and broken, never to be repaired. Within days of the graveyard he looked old; his hair snow white, his face wizened like he'd seen a lifetime happen in one night; and in a sense he had. He spends his days now looking out the window for the dark nothingness which will surely come for him. After all, he was there the night it showed itself.

Foster left the agency after the death of Cal Denver. In all his years in the police and in the agency, he had never witnessed anything the like of what he'd seen in the graveyard that night. So he withdrew from the shadows and lived in the light. He relocated his entire life to Hawaii, to the beaches and sun of some imaginary paradise. The itch for mystery would never leave him though. Once in a while he checked in on young Jade as she grew into womanhood. Speaking to her had one down side. He was soon sucked into what had become her world, filled with shadows. He would never be the same again.

Jade had been forced to leave, her mother too spooked by the events to stay. But she soon came back, unable to resist the pull of the town, almost like her story had begun there and not quite ended. She became the crazy lady in town, the one whose house children would dare each other to approach on Halloween for cheap scares. Her friends were as good as their promise; they wouldn't leave until she was ready.

Sometimes she would go out with sprays of wildflowers to place on their graves. Occasionally she would dance around them like she was in the midst of a host of party goers. If she had been seen, the townsfolk would have had their suspicions of madness confirmed as she twirled with hands aloft, a beatific smile playing across her lips, but they didn't see as she saw.

She had invited darkness into her life and it had invaded her, but her friends would watch over her for as long as she needed them to be there. They would fight back the shadows which would, from the day of her minor spell making to the time she joined them in death, stalk her very soul. Her burial of the grimoire alongside Tommy's body would not appease those dark beings.

And so, night after night she looked toward the graveyard where they lay, all within a few feet of each other, and smiled.

The dead stayed dead. They were happier that way.

55329743R00115

Made in the USA
Charleston, SC
23 April 2016